MONTANA MAVERICKS

Welcome to Big Sky Country, home of the Montana Mavericks! Where free-spirited men and women discover love on the range.

THE REAL COWBOYS OF BRONCO HEIGHTS

The young people of Bronco are so busy with their careers—and their ranches!—that they have pushed all thoughts of love to the back burner. Elderly Winona Cobbs knows full well what it is like to live a life that is only half-full. And she resolves to help them see the error of their ways...

The crowds cheer whenever Geoff Burris steps into the rodeo ring, and he has always appreciated his fans. Now, though, he has met a woman who doesn't care that he is a star. Stephanie sees the real man behind the cowboy hat and he thinks she could be The One. But what if keeping Stephanie means sacrificing the fame he has worked so hard to achieve?

Dear Reader,

I've never been much of a celebrity follower. I don't know who is married to whom, who is cheating with whom or who is the latest "it" couple. I don't know which stars are engaged in a Twitter battle or who has kissed and made up. Even so, I was intrigued by the idea of writing a celebrity romance.

What would it be like to date one of the most famous athletes in the country? I had fun answering this question while writing *A Kiss at the Mistletoe Rodeo*.

Geoff Burris has worked hard for the success he's achieved. The face of rodeo, he lives his life in a fishbowl. Although he appreciates his fans, he wouldn't mind a few days out of the spotlight. When he returns to his hometown to host Bronco's inaugural Mistletoe Rodeo, he plans to reconnect with old friends and enjoy some of his mom's home cooking.

What he didn't plan on was falling for Stephanie Brandt, a local girl who loves working as a nurse. Stephanie's not looking for fame or fortune, or a place in the spotlight. But when Geoff comes along, she is torn between her feelings for him and the quiet life she has always lived.

I loved watching these two resist falling in love. I hope you enjoy Geoff and Stephanie's romance as much as I enjoyed writing it.

I love hearing from my readers. Feel free to stop by my website, kathydouglassbooks.com, and leave me a message. While you're there, sign up for my monthly newsletter. You can also find me on Facebook, Twitter, BookBub and Instagram.

Thank you for your support.

Happy reading!

Kathy

A Kiss at the Mistletoe Rodeo

KATHY DOUGLASS

HARLEQUIN

SPECIAL
EDITION

Special thanks and acknowledgment are given to Kathy Douglass
for her contribution to the Montana Mavericks:
The Real Cowboys of Bronco Heights miniseries.

HARLEQUIN®
SPECIAL
EDITION™

Recycling programs
for this product may
not exist in your area.

ISBN-13: 978-1-335-40816-7

A Kiss at the Mistletoe Rodeo

Harlequin Enterprises ULC
22 Adelaide St. West, 40th Floor
Toronto, Ontario M5H 4E3, Canada
www.Harlequin.com

Printed in U.S.A.

Kathy Douglass came by her love of reading naturally—both of her parents were readers. She would finish one book and pick up another. Then she attended law school and traded romances for legal opinions.

After the birth of her two children, her love of reading turned into a love of writing. Kathy now spends her days writing the small-town contemporary novels she enjoys reading.

Books by Kathy Douglass

Harlequin Special Edition

Sweet Briar Sweethearts

How to Steal the Lawman's Heart
The Waitress's Secret
The Rancher and the City Girl
Winning Charlotte Back
The Rancher's Return
A Baby Between Friends
The Single Mom's Second Chance
The Soldier Under Her Tree
Redemption on Rivers Ranch

Furever Yours

The City Girl's Homecoming

Montana Mavericks: What Happened to Beatrix?

The Maverick's Baby Arrangement

Visit the Author Profile page
at Harlequin.com for more titles.

Chapter One

"What do you think?" Katy, the assistant to the manager of the Bronco Convention Center, turned her wide eyes to Geoff Burris as her spirited tour came to an end. "It's really something, right?"

The newly remodeled arena was state-of-the-art, and Katy had shown it off, everything from the bull and bronco pens to the dressing rooms for the contestants, the press booth, the VIP booths above the general seating, and even the areas for meet and greets with rodeo fans. The organizers of the Mistletoe Rodeo had thought of everything.

"Yes," Geoff agreed. "Everything looks perfect."

The inaugural Mistletoe Rodeo was scheduled to be held in two weeks. Amateurs as well as professionals would be showing off their skills in the three-day event. According to Geoff's mother, the entire town of Bronco had been looking forward to the event ever since it had been announced that Geoff would be participating.

The young woman smiled brightly. She'd been beaming at Geoff ever since Chuck Carter, the manager of the convention center, had introduced them that morning. After shaking Geoff's hand, Mr. Carter had returned to his on-site office, leaving Geoff in what he described as the capable hands of his assistant. Katy had practically glued herself to Geoff's side as she'd spent the past forty-five minutes gushing about the venue to Geoff and the entourage of local and national press. Geoff was used to dealing with enthusiastic fans, but somehow, he'd expected things to be different in Bronco. After all, he'd grown up here. His parents still lived in the same house he and his three younger brothers had been raised in.

Geoff had been on the rodeo circuit for nearly half of his thirty-two years and had met with almost instant success as a bronc rider. Most of his time was spent on the road and away from his hometown, so he was glad to be back in Bronco for the next month or so. He'd missed home. He was looking forward to enjoying his mother's cooking and catching up with old friends. It would be a welcome change to be around people who didn't fawn over him, but treated him as one of the guys.

"This is a big deal for Bronco," Katy added. "Having you and other big rodeo stars participate is going to do wonders for our town. I'm so excited I can barely stand it. My heart is practically jumping out of my chest." She slid a hand over her tight sweater as if attempting to draw his attention to her breasts. To be fair, she had a nice enough figure, but he wasn't interested. Not that he didn't date. He did. Extensively. But he kept things casual and everything about this woman screamed Velcro. If he gave her even the slightest indication that he was open to seeing her, he'd never get away from her. Since he didn't enjoy hurting people and did everything he could to prevent it, he had to keep everything between them strictly professional. He couldn't even crack a smile for fear that she would take it as encouragement.

"I'm looking forward to it." Although he knew that his words were being recorded, both by the journalists following him as well as the television crews who'd been on his trail seemingly forever—or at least since he won the state bronc riding contest in junior high—he meant every word he said. He was looking forward to participating in the Mistletoe Rodeo.

Acting as master of ceremonies as well as competing in the rodeo gave him the best of both worlds. He was able to participate in a sport he loved, and he was home for the holidays, something that was rare for him. He'd arrived in town two days ago. His brothers, who were also on the rodeo tour and would be competing in the Mistletoe Rodeo, would be arriving in about ten days. Geoff was looking forward to restarting their years-long ping-pong tournament they had with their father. Their father always won, but Geoff never gave up hope that either he or one of his brothers would dethrone him.

"How about we take a couple of pictures over there?" Curtis, the photographer for the *Bronco Bulletin*, asked, pointing at the stands.

"Sure." Geoff quickly excused himself and then jogged over to the stands. "Where do you want me?"

"Climb up to the top. Then hold your arms out as if surveying the land or something. You know. Kind of master of all you survey."

Shaking his head at the idea, Geoff jogged up the steps two at a time. When he reached the top, he spun around and posed as directed. Over the years, he'd done plenty of interviews and photo shoots, but he'd never quite understood being famous. It amazed him that people were interested in his life and had his pictures hanging on their walls. Of course, as a teenaged boy, he'd had his heroes' posters on his bedroom walls, but that was different. Bill Pickett and Nat Love had been trailblazers. Legends. Bill Pickett had actually invented bulldogging, the skill of grabbing steer by the horns and wrestling them to the ground. And Nat Love was one of the most famous heroes of the old west. He, on the other hand, was just Geoff Burris, son of Jeanne and Benjamin Burris. Brother of Jack, Ross and Mike Burris.

Curtis took pictures from different angles, calling out instructions nonstop. Geoff was so busy listening to the photographer's directions that he didn't pay as close attention as he should have to where he stepped. One minute the bleacher was beneath his boot and he was smiling at the camera as directed. The next he was in midair, arms flailing as he tried in vain to regain his balance.

Geoff heard Katy's bloodcurdling scream as he thudded onto the concrete floor. The fall knocked the wind out of him and he gasped, doing his best to suck in oxygen. After a long, nervous minute, he was able to breathe normally.

Then everyone began to talk at once as they ran over to him. Geoff tried to sit up and let them know he was okay, but as he raised his arm, intense pain forced him to stop.

"I called 911," Katy said as she knelt by his side. "An ambulance should be here soon."

"Thanks."

"Can you stand?" Curtis asked, putting down his camera and extending a hand.

"I think so."

Geoff tried to move his leg and his right ankle screamed in agony. As his adrenaline faded, he realized that his entire body was in excruciating pain.

"You should wait until the paramedics check you out."

"Did you hit your head?" someone else asked.

"No," Geoff replied. At least he didn't think he did. It all happened so fast.

"What happened?" That question came from Mr. Carter, who'd apparently heard the noise and had raced into the arena, loudly demanding answers. People began to talk at once, saying what they'd witnessed or hypothesizing about the cause. The cacophony made Geoff's head pound and he gave up trying to answer. There was nothing that needed saying at this point anyway. Most of the answers were self-evident. He'd fallen from the bleachers and injured himself.

The sound of approaching sirens temporarily silenced the growing crowd of onlookers.

Two EMTs arrived and jogged across the floor, pulling a wheeled gurney behind them. One, a woman with alert brown eyes, asked him his name.

"He's Geoff Burris," Katy said, taking his hand.

"Ma'am, would you mind stepping back?" the EMT said. "And we need for him to answer the questions."

"My name is Geoff Burris," Geoff replied.

"Can you tell me what happened?" the woman asked as her partner wrapped the blood pressure cuff around his biceps and expertly inflated it.

He moved his head to meet her gaze and a sharp pain between his eyes made him wince, reminding him to be more careful when he moved. "I was standing on top of the bleachers taking pictures. I thought the bleacher was longer than it was. I must have missed a step, and I fell."

"I see."

"I'm not hurt all that badly. I just got banged up a little bit. Give me a few minutes to shake it off and I'll be fine." After a lifetime as a bronc rider, he'd suffered his share of injuries. Most people in rodeo had. You couldn't go to the hospital for every little bump or bruise.

"I hate to disagree with you, but you need to go to the hospital and get checked out."

He thought about his mother hearing about him being rushed to the hospital in an ambulance and cringed. Jeanne had always worried about her sons getting hurt in the rodeo. Although she'd always supported them in whatever they chose to do, he knew she would be happier if they'd become architects or accountants. She'd been thrilled when Mike told her he planned to become a doctor. That thrill had worn off when he'd told her he would be earning his medical school tuition by joining his brothers on the rodeo circuit. Of course Geoff had gotten hurt while taking pictures, something that was supposed to be safer than rodeo. This freak accident only bolstered his belief that he could just as easily be hurt crossing the street as being tossed from a bucking bronc.

"I don't need an ambulance. I can call for a car."

He used his good hand to pull his phone from his back pocket. It had been smashed.

"Nonsense," Mr. Carter said, coming to squat next to Geoff's shoulder. Thankfully he'd stopped yelling even if he hadn't stopped giving orders. "You take the ambulance to the hospital and let the doctors take care of you." He then turned his focus to the EMTs. "And you get him there as soon as you can. Lights and sirens."

The EMT who'd been taking Geoff's vitals frowned, but otherwise didn't react to Mr. Carter. No doubt he'd run into all types in his job. Geoff didn't want to make things more difficult for the young man who was only doing his job, so he stopped protesting.

"Okay. Can someone grab my jacket?"

Mr. Carter snapped his fingers and Katy immediately began searching for Geoff's belongings. Geoff was about to tell her to forget about it when she returned with the shearling jacket.

"Thank you," Geoff said as he was assisted onto the gurney. In the blink of an eye, the EMTs had him covered with a blanket and strapped in. Geoff stared at the ceiling as they wheeled him through the center. When he started getting dizzy and his stomach lurched, he closed his eyes. Luckily the nausea vanished by the time he was placed inside the ambulance.

With the added advantage—if one could call

it that—of the blaring sirens, the ride to the hospital was short and in no time Geoff found himself being transferred onto a bed in the emergency room.

The doctor, a man who looked to be in his early fifties and whose name tag identified him as Dr. Shaw, peered at Geoff over rimless glasses. "So, you had a bit of an accident at the convention center. I expected to have a few visits from you rodeo types, but not for a couple of weeks."

Geoff wasn't surprised that the doctor recognized him. His success on the tour brought plenty of endorsement opportunities ranging from belt buckles to shirts and ties. He'd recently done an ad campaign for BH Couture, a local boutique, and signed a sponsorship and advertising deal with Taylor Beef, another local business, and would be shooting some commercials while he was in town.

Geoff had been reluctant to advertise products when he first started out, wanting to be known for his exploits in the ring, not outside of it. But once he'd made a name for himself in his sport, his stance had changed. His name recognition had created more interest in rodeo, and he'd taken advantage of the opportunity to spread the word whenever and however he could.

The sponsorship opportunities were also very lucrative, which enabled him to help those he loved as well as support worthy causes. It was a win-

win situation and the best use of his fame that he could think of.

"I'm part of the advance crew. I just wanted to make sure the medical staff was up to par," Geoff said with a wry grin.

Dr. Shaw chuckled. "You could have just asked to tour the facilities."

"I didn't think of that."

The doctor nodded and then, all joking behind them, reached out and touched Geoff's arm.

Geoff sucked in a pained breath.

After attempting to manipulate the arm and shoulder, the doctor looked at Geoff with serious eyes. "I have a feeling you're going to need surgery on that shoulder."

"Surgery? Are you sure?" That would ruin everything.

The doctor made a notation on the chart. "I'm ordering X-rays to confirm my diagnosis, but yes, I'm sure."

"What do you think is wrong?"

"Looks like you might have dislocated your shoulder."

"That's not a big deal. I've dislocated my shoulder a couple of times in the past. It just needs to be popped in."

"Well, see, that's the problem. If you dislocate your shoulder more than once, the ligaments need to be surgically repaired."

"If I need surgery, how long will it take to recover?"

"Depends on how extensive the repair is."

"What's your best guess?"

"I'm not a surgeon, but ballpark… I'd say you'll be in a sling for at least four to six weeks."

"Four to six weeks! I'm participating in the Mistletoe Rodeo in two weeks."

"I wouldn't count on it."

Geoff inhaled and the doctor raised a hand, stopping him from speaking. "Let's wait and see what the surgeon has to say before you get all worked up, shall we?"

Geoff nodded. It didn't make sense to get all stressed out when he didn't know how bad things were.

The doctor examined Geoff's ankle. "That's probably just a bad sprain, but I'll order X-rays to be on the safe side. And of course I'll order a scan of your head just to be sure you don't have a concussion. Sit tight and someone will be in to take you for your tests."

Geoff nodded absently as the doctor left, preoccupied by thoughts of his injured shoulder. He couldn't be laid up for a month. He had commitments to keep.

He was still brooding over the doctor's words twenty minutes later when the curtain surrounding his bed was pulled back.

"I'm here to take you for your tests," an orderly said, pushing an empty wheelchair up to the bed. "Are you ready?"

"Ready as I'll ever be," he replied.

The young man looked at Geoff's face and then his mouth dropped open. He pointed a finger at Geoff. "You're Geoff Burris."

"Yes, I am."

"I'm a big fan."

"Thanks."

The young man stared at Geoff for a long moment. Then, as if realizing he had a job to do, he shook his head and helped Geoff into the wheelchair. The orderly talked excitedly about the upcoming Mistletoe Rodeo as he pushed Geoff down the hall to the radiology department. "I'm taking my girlfriend on the final night. We've already got our tickets. We're both big fans and always watch when rodeo comes on TV, but we always wanted to see you in person. We'd been talking about taking a trip to see you on the road, but this is so much better. You're still going to ride, aren't you?"

"Of course. I wouldn't want to let down my fans." People were paying good money to see him participate and he wasn't going to disappoint them. After years of performing around the country in stadiums filled with strangers, he wasn't going to let a dislocated shoulder stop him from performing before a crowd filled with friends and relatives.

The X-rays and scan didn't take long and soon Geoff was back in the emergency room cooling his heels. A little while later, Dr. Shaw entered. "What do you want first, the good news or the bad news?"

"How about you give me the good and we skip the bad altogether?"

The doctor shook his head. "If only it were that easy. But not hearing the report won't change the facts. The good news is that your ankle isn't broken. You just have a sprain. You should be back on your feet in a few days."

"That is good news."

"And there's more. You don't have a concussion."

"That's not surprising given that I didn't hit my head." No doubt his headache was the result of too many loud voices in the arena, coupled with the rush of adrenaline.

The doctor paused.

Geoff sighed. "I take it we've run out of good news."

Dr. Shaw nodded. "I'm afraid so. You've done substantial damage to your shoulder and the X-rays confirm that you need surgery to repair the tendons. Lucky for you, Dr. Wilson, one of the best orthopedists in the state, is a part of our hospital system. I've already checked and he's available to perform your surgery tomorrow morning."

"Is surgery really necessary? Can't you just

give me a splint and some painkillers and let me go home?"

"That's out of the question."

"How about a cast, then?" He didn't know how he would compete with one arm in a cast, but he'd find a way. What he wasn't going to do was have surgery tomorrow or any other day.

"I'm sorry, Mr. Burris. I don't think you understand just how much damage you did. If you don't take care of this now, you'll be in pain for the rest of your life. Not only that, but you won't be able to perform at your current level. Is that what you want?"

Of course it wasn't what Geoff wanted. He didn't want to be less than he was. He knew that eventually Father Time would catch up to him and he'd lose his strength and the ability to make lightning-fast adjustments. Eventually someone would come along and knock him off the top spot. That was the nature of rodeo. The nature of life. But that time wasn't *now*. He wasn't going to allow a photo shoot gone wrong to derail him at the peak of his career.

"Fine. I'll have the surgery." But there was no way he was going to sit around and do nothing for weeks. For as long as he could remember, his father had told him that a man was only as good as his word. Geoff had made a promise to the rodeo promoters and he was going to keep it.

"Good." The doctor handed Geoff some tablets. "Now that we've established that you don't have a concussion, we can give you some medication for the pain."

"Thanks." Geoff didn't like to take much, but he knew there was nothing manly or heroic about refusing medicine that could ease his pain. Besides, he couldn't focus with his body in such misery. He swallowed the pills and hoped they'd kick in soon.

"I'll have someone take you to registration so we can get you checked in."

"I need to contact my parents, too."

"We can do that."

"Thanks." Geoff would have preferred to go to his parents' house where he could sleep in his own bed, but he knew it was probably best to spend the night in the hospital. That way nobody would have to drive him back here in the morning for surgery. Besides, he didn't think he could stand looking in his mother's eyes and seeing the worry there. He might be a grown man, but she still considered him and his brothers her babies.

Checking in took a bit longer than Geoff would have liked, and by the time he was escorted to his private room, the pain medicine had begun to kick in. On the plus side, he was feeling no pain. On the negative side, he was feeling a bit loopy.

The orderly wheeled him up beside the bed and then stepped back. Geoff attempted to stand when he felt a hand on his shoulder. "Careful. You don't want to hurt your ankle. Let me help you."

The feminine voice startled him. The orderly had been a man, so Geoff knew he hadn't spoken. Geoff turned his head and stared at the most beautiful woman he'd ever seen. Brown skin and almond-shaped eyes that were at once intelligent and kind. High cheekbones. Full, kissable lips. As she wrapped her arms around him, helping him to stand on his one good leg while she steered him onto the bed, he knew she had to be an angel. An angel sent down from heaven to help him through the night.

He smiled. He liked the sound of that.

"You like the sound of what?" his angel asked. Her voice was melodic. Sweet yet sexy. The kind of voice that could talk a man into doing anything.

"Whatever you want, angel." He sat docilely while she helped him into a hospital gown. Then he lay back against the pillow, and she covered him with the thin blanket.

"Just how much medicine did they give you?" that sexy voice asked.

"Not sure."

"Well, you should be able to sleep."

As she turned to leave, he grabbed her arm. "Stay, angel. Don't leave."

Nurse Stephanie Brandt looked at her patient. Although he'd been registered as Bernie Jefferson, she easily recognized Geoff Burris, champion rodeo star and hometown hero. Although she wasn't a sports fan, you couldn't live in Bronco, Montana, and not know of the living legend that was Geoff Burris. He was by far the most famous person to come from this Montana town and was the favorite son. Now that he was representing Taylor Beef, she expected to see his face on her television screen, billboards and print advertisement even more often.

And what a face it was. Geoff Burris was quite a handsome man. With clear brown skin, chiseled cheekbones and strong jaw, he was more gorgeous than the patients Stephanie ordinarily encountered. And his body! Words like *muscular* didn't come close to describing it. He was tall and lean without an ounce of excess fat. Clearly being a rodeo star required more strength than she'd thought. He was obviously an elite athlete in his prime. While helping him change out of his street clothes and into his hospital gown, she'd seen firsthand just how fit he was.

The temptation to stroke her hand over the smooth skin covering his six-pack abs had been strong, but it would have been entirely inappropriate and unprofessional. And Stephanie was nothing if not professional. She was a nurse and he was her patient. As such, he deserved her best care—

which didn't include being gawked at like an animal in a zoo.

"What is it that you need?" she asked her sleepy patient.

His eyes had drifted shut. With apparent effort, he opened them and blinked several times before he managed to meet her eyes. "I need you, angel."

Her heart lurched at his words, and it took all of her self-control to not melt into a puddle right then and there. She frowned at that thought. She wasn't some groupie who got weak in the knees at some no doubt well-rehearsed, oft-repeated line. "What you need is rest."

He reached out and grabbed her wrist with a speed that was shocking. "Don't go, I need you."

She gently unwrapped his fingers from her wrist and placed his hand on top of the blanket. "I have to go now. My shift is over. But don't worry, you won't be alone. There are other nurses who will take good care of you." Though she didn't know why, she added, "I promise to come back tomorrow and check on you."

He nodded and his eyes closed again. "I didn't know angels worked shifts."

Since he'd already fallen asleep, Stephanie didn't bother to reply. She didn't know what she would have said anyway. After an unusually busy shift, she was exhausted and her brain was barely functioning. All she wanted to do was get home, heat up the leftovers her mother had insisted that she take home after Sunday dinner, and veg out in front of the television for a couple of hours.

Stephanie went into the nurses' locker room where she changed out of her scrubs and into a comfy pair of jeans and a thick green sweater. She pulled on a matching green coat and wound a scarf around her neck before going to the nurses' station and saying goodbye.

"Have a good night," Tamara, her friend and favorite coworker, said, glancing up from a file and taking a sip of coffee.

"Thanks. You, too."

Stephanie stepped through the hospital doors and was immediately hit by a blast of cold air. She sucked in a bracing breath. Montana might be among the most beautiful places in the country, and she couldn't imagine living anywhere else, but she found the cold weather challenging. She wrapped the scarf more tightly around her neck and then put on her green fur-lined leather gloves before striding to the parking lot. As she neared her car, she spotted someone approaching her. The overhead lights provided decent lighting, but the figure was mostly in shadows. As the person got closer, Stephanie was able to make out the figure. Winona Cobbs. Stephanie had learned about the older woman last year when the Abernathys, one of Bronco's wealthier families, were seeking information about Winona's biological daughter who had been taken away at birth. Stephanie didn't recall all of the details, but she knew it had been a big deal and that Winona had eventually been happily reunited with Dorothea "Daisy" McGowan.

"Hello," Stephanie said when they were close enough to hear each other without shouting. "Do you need help?"

Winona shook her head. "I'm here to visit a friend."

"Okay," Stephanie replied and continued walking to her car, which brought her closer to Winona. When they were within inches of passing each other, Winona stepped in front of Stephanie and placed her frail hands on her shoulders. Her fingers might have been bony, but her hold on Stephanie was firm. Tight. "You can run, but you can't hide."

"I beg your pardon." Stephanie stepped back and looked at Winona. Her eyes were clear and she didn't appear to be under the influence of alcohol—or anything else. Still, her words didn't make any sense. "I have no idea what you're talking about. Perhaps you've mistaken me for someone else."

"Oh, I know exactly who you are. I'm here to let you know it's useless to resist. The rodeo rider has already lassoed your heart."

Stephanie froze at Winona's words and internally she shivered. Stephanie had never been a big believer in second sight or intuition or any other woo-woo things, preferring to trust in science and logic, but Winona's words were a little bit uncanny. Unnerving. How had Winona known Stephanie had a rodeo rider as a patient? Geoff had been admitted under a false name to protect his privacy so she couldn't have confirmed he was a patient by calling the hospital. Even if she knew Geoff had been admitted, there was no way Winona could have known that Stephanie and Geoff had met. This was all too weird.

"I don't know what you mean," Stephanie said, shaking her head.

"Oh, I think you do. But I guess you're entitled to live in denial for a little while longer. Most people prefer it there. But you can't stay too long."

"What?"

Winona laughed. "Everything I'm saying will make perfect sense to you in a little while. Have a nice night now." Without saying another word, Winona continued walking to the hospital, presumably to visit her friend as if she hadn't just said the most befuddling thing Stephanie had ever heard.

Although the wind whipped through the parking lot, chilling Stephanie to the bone, she didn't resume walking. It was as if the old woman's words had left her spellbound. Sure, Geoff Burris was handsome. Stephanie had known that before she'd walked into his room. She'd seen his face on TV and billboards around Montana for years. But those images had failed to fully capture his good looks. More than that, they'd been unable to reveal his essence. Even with painkillers, he still possessed a certain magnetism that naturally drew people—and certainly women—to him. And when he had called her *angel*… Whew. Despite the cold Montana air swirling around her, Stephanie began to perspire. Of course he hadn't meant anything by it. People said all kinds of wacky things when they were under the influence of painkillers. Besides, patients often referred to their nurses as angels, so thankful for the little things nurses did to make their recovery more pleasant.

So why was she standing out here thinking about him all the while freezing her butt off instead of getting in her car and driving home?

The wind blew especially hard, shaking Stephanie out of her stupor, and she jogged the rest of the way to her car. Once inside she turned on the heat and pressed her hands to her freezing face. What had possessed her to stand outside in the cold like that? Winona's words may have been odd, but they held no more truth than a fortune cookie.

Grateful for the heated seats warming her chilled bottom, she drove to her house. Stephanie was one of five children and had grown up in a close, loving family. Though she enjoyed their company, and had enjoyed sharing a room with her younger sister Tiffany for most of her life, she liked having her own place and decorating it in her own personal style.

After parking in her driveway, she opened the door to her two-bedroom house. She'd grown up in Bronco Valley, but happened to luck out and find an affordable home for sale in Bronco Heights, the more well-to-do side of town. Stephanie liked bold, dramatic colors. The deep blue chairs and sofa with white accent pillows and throws combined with the blue-and-gray wallpaper generally made her smile and relax as soon as she stepped inside. But as she dropped onto the padded bench to exchange her boots for fuzzy slippers, the tension from the day didn't slip from her shoulders.

As they had on the drive home, Winona's words echoed through her mind, although Stephanie couldn't figure out why she was giving them so much attention. Winona was known around town to be a bit eccentric. Although Stephanie had been raised to know better than to spread gossip, that didn't keep her from hearing it. Or from observing people with her own eyes. Truthfully, given everything she knew about Winona, Stephanie wouldn't be giving the older woman's words a second thought if she didn't see a little bit of truth in them.

Geoff might not have lassoed her heart; it took more than a gorgeous face and muscular body to do that. But he had definitely gotten her attention. And maybe she was a little bit attracted to him. But even so, they lived in two different worlds. He was a celebrity and she was a nurse. Just because their worlds had collided today didn't mean there would be a long-term connection.

She was a simple girl living a simple life. Sure, she appreciated the finer things—dinner in a nice restaurant, a good bottle of wine and exquisite jewelry that she saw in the window of Beaumont and Rossi's Fine Jewels. But when it came to her everyday life, she preferred spending a quiet evening with friends or family, soaking in her oversized tub while listening to her favorite singers, and watching sci-fi reruns on TV. She had no desire to live in the limelight.

Geoff's life was nothing like hers. He was constantly photographed and followed by hordes of fans. He didn't have any privacy to speak of. There was nothing quiet about his life. Not that it mattered. He was her patient. When he was released from the hospital, she wouldn't see him again.

Chapter Two

"Do you need anything?"

Geoff looked into his mother's eyes. Although she'd spoken in what he'd always thought of as her kindergarten teacher voice, he heard the worry behind her calm tone. Dr. Shaw had instructed someone to contact his parents shortly after he'd been admitted, and they had arrived at the hospital a little while after his angel had left.

His brothers had heard about his accident on the news and had rushed to his side. The media had embellished the story and exaggerated his injuries, so they'd been frantic by the time they'd arrived last night. They'd half expected him to be on life support instead of trying to sleep in the uncomfortable bed.

"Nope."

"Jeanne," Geoff's father said, patting his mother's hand, "there's nothing you can get him. He's going into surgery in a few minutes."

"Of course. I know that. I just forgot."

His mother looked so frazzled that Geoff immediately felt guilty for worrying her. Although in his defense he hadn't intended to get hurt. He'd been so focused on the photographer's instructions that he hadn't been as aware of where he'd been standing as he should have been. "There is one thing that I do need."

"What is it?" his mother asked.

"I could use a hug."

Without saying a word, his mother leaned over and pulled him into her perfumed embrace. For a minute he was four years old again and had fallen out of a tree, spraining his ankle. Back then he'd tried to maintain a stiff upper lip, but after taking two steps he'd crumbled to the ground, crying. His mother had wrapped him in a tight embrace and kissed his wet cheek. Although her touch hadn't taken away the pain, he'd known instantly that everything would be okay. Now he'd only asked for the hug in order to make her feel better, but her touch did ease the slight worry lurking in the back of his mind.

After a long moment, his mother pulled back and looked at him. Her eyes no longer glistened with unshed tears. Instead, they were filled with determination. "You're going to be fine."

"I know. I have a great doctor and the surgery is simple." He repeated the words that had been told to him, first by the emergency room doctor last night, then echoed by the nurses this morning, and finally by the surgeon himself.

A nurse walked into the room, a bright smile on her face although it wasn't even 6:00 a.m. yet. "Are you ready?"

"I am." Geoff looked over at his parents. "I'll see you later."

"You bet. We'll be waiting outside for you." His father gave his good shoulder a squeeze and his mother kissed his cheek.

Geoff watched his parents leave the room to join his brothers in the family waiting area. Unlike his parents, once his brothers had known he hadn't been seriously injured, they'd teased him about getting hurt.

"Way to avoid competing," Mike had joked to the amusement of his other brothers. Despite their kidding, Geoff had known they'd been concerned about him.

Geoff had laughed along last night, but now he worried that the injury would keep him from competing. All of the promotions had included his name and picture. He was the headliner.

"Hey, why the frown? Dr. Wilson is one of the best in the nation."

Geoff glanced at the nurse and smiled, trying to take comfort in her words and not focus on the worst-case scenario. Brooding wouldn't change the outcome. "I know."

She wheeled him down the hall and into an elevator. When they reached the surgical floor, he was taken to the presurgical room where a surgical nurse took over.

"You'll be going to surgery in a few minutes. I'm going to give you a mild sedative to help you relax. When you get to the OR, you'll receive anesthesia. When the surgery is over, you'll be taken to the recovery room. Your family will be able to see you once you're awake. Sound good?"

"Yes." As if he had a choice in the matter.

Someone wheeled him into the operating room. And then everything went black.

Geoff heard the beeping of machines and the murmur of voices, forced his eyes open and looked around. It took a couple of minutes for his mind to clear and for him to get his bearings. He'd just had surgery and was in the recovery room. He looked down at his arm. It was wrapped in bandages and a sling.

"Well, look who's waking up."

Geoff looked at the nurse. "How long have I been asleep?"

"About two hours. I think that might be a combination of the anesthesia and just being sleepy."

That was possible since he hadn't slept well last night. "How did the surgery go?"

"It went well. The doctor has spoken with your parents. He'll be by to speak with you later."

"Thanks."

"Your family is still waiting. If you want, I'll let them know you're awake so they can come and visit you."

He nodded and closed his eyes again. After a brief visit with his family, Geoff was returned to his room. He was more alert by then and even with a bum ankle he didn't need assistance getting back into the bed. "When will the doctor be in to see me?"

The nurse checked his vitals before she answered. "He's in surgery. But don't worry, he'll be in before long."

Geoff nodded. Most of the anesthesia had worn off by then and he was no longer groggy. He'd insisted that his family go home, saying there was no reason for them to sit around for hours while they waited for him to be discharged. He would call his brother Mike for a ride home when he was released. It had taken some urging because his mother was determined to stay by his side. She'd only agreed to leave after Geoff had said he had a taste for her chicken and dumplings for dinner.

Now he was getting antsy and wanted to leave himself. He was reaching for the buzzer to call the nurse when Dr. Wilson stepped into the room.

"How's the arm?"

Geoff grimaced. "You'd know better than I would."

The doctor chuckled. "True enough. Surgery went well. I expect you to make a full recovery. Now all you need to do is rest."

"Which I plan to do the minute I get out of here. What time do you think I'll be released today?"

"Today? You're not going to be released today. You just had open reconstructive shoulder surgery. You need to stay the night for observation. You'll be released tomorrow morning at the earliest."

"No way," Geoff said, springing into a sitting position. His arm didn't appreciate being jostled and pain shot through his body and his eyes watered. He blinked back the moisture and ignored the pain. "I can't stay here overnight."

"You don't have a choice. We need to monitor your recovery."

"No." A part of Geoff knew that he was being irrational, but he couldn't help it. He wanted to go home.

"Son, you came to me for help and I gave it to you. You needed surgery and I did the best job that I could. But you also have a role to play in your recovery. In order to give yourself the best chance to heal, you need to stay here overnight. And when you leave here, you need to rest that arm for a while."

"The rodeo is in two weeks." He'd already told that to the emergency room doctor. Perhaps the message hadn't been relayed to the surgeon. "I need to be there. I'm the master of ceremonies."

"And you can still be the master of ceremonies. As long as that's all you do."

That wasn't Geoff's plan, but he wasn't going to argue about that now. He'd made a commitment and he intended to keep it. "I don't want to stay the night. I can sleep at my parents' house."

"Tomorrow you can do that. But the nurses need to keep watch over you for the rest of the day and tonight."

Geoff realized this was a battle he wasn't going to win. "Okay. I'll stay. But the only nurse I'll allow in this room is the angel from last night."

"Angel? What angel?" The doctor looked confused. "Did you see this angel before or after your pain medicine?"

"I didn't imagine her if that's what you're getting at. I wasn't hallucinating. She was real," Geoff insisted. True, she seemed too sweet to be real, too beautiful to not be a celestial being, but he knew she was a flesh-and-blood woman because they'd touched.

"What was her name?"

Geoff wasn't sure whether the doctor was humoring him, but he chose to give the man the benefit of the doubt. "I don't know. I didn't ask her for it."

"I see. Well, all of our nurses are professionals

who give the highest quality care. I'm sure you'll be satisfied with whoever is assigned to you."

Geoff shook his head. This was nonnegotiable. If he was going to be held captive in this hospital, there was only one nurse he wanted. "No. I want my angel."

The doctor raised his eyebrows, and Geoff wondered if perhaps the anesthesia hadn't completely worn off. That was the only thing that could account for his stubborn insistence. He blew out a breath. "I'm not going to harass her or anything if that's what you're worried about. I'm not that kind of man. She was just a good nurse and I prefer to have her care for me as opposed to having to get used to someone else. And the fewer people who know I'm here, the better chance I'll have of maintaining my privacy and getting the rest you say I need to recover."

After a moment, Dr. Wilson nodded. "What did she look like?"

Geoff closed his eyes and pictured the woman. "She was absolutely beautiful."

The doctor laughed. "I'm going to need you to be a little more specific."

"She had beautiful clear brown skin, and high cheekbones like a cover model. Her eyes were deep brown. Almost black. Like a cup of coffee with just a dab of cream. And her lips…" Geoff caught himself a second before he sighed.

Her lips had been kissable, but he wasn't going to say *that*. He didn't want to give the doctor the wrong idea. Heck, he didn't want to give himself the wrong idea. "You could tell that she smiled a lot. She was really friendly. Very nice."

The doctor stared hard at Geoff as if assessing his character. Geoff knew that many athletes had bad reputations, but he'd been careful to behave in the manner consistent with the way he'd been raised. His parents had expected him and his brothers to be respectful and to uphold the good name they'd been given at birth. And he had. He'd never let his fame or fortune go to his head and he would never do anything to besmirch the Burris family name.

Dr. Wilson must have liked what he'd seen because after a minute he nodded. "Fine. I'll speak with the nursing supervisor. If your nurse is working today, we can assign her to your room."

Geoff relaxed and he realized he'd been tense as he'd waited for the doctor's answer. He didn't know how or why this nurse had become so important to him, or why he needed to see her again, but some things were inexplicable. Apparently this was one of them. "Thank you. I appreciate it."

The doctor nodded and left the room, returning a minute later with a no-nonsense-looking woman whom Geoff assumed was the nursing supervisor. She wasn't smiling, and Geoff had a feeling that she didn't appreciate the special request. He acknowledged that he might look like a prima donna, but that wasn't the case at all.

As his popularity and bank accounts had grown, he'd encountered many unscrupulous people and his willingness to trust had taken a hit. He was wary of letting new people into his life and kept only a tight circle of friends. He'd made mistakes in the early years, but he'd finally learned to trust his gut. And his gut was telling him that his angel-nurse could be trusted. He couldn't say why, but he just had a sense that he wouldn't have to worry about her secretly taking pictures of him and selling them to the press or posting them on her social media accounts.

The supervisor pressed her lips together, disapproval radiating from her every pore. "Dr. Wilson relayed your request. It sounds like you're talking about Stephanie Brandt."

"That could be her. She didn't tell me her name," he said, realizing how foolish he must sound. Describing her this way was only slightly better than pulling a glass slipper out of his bag and having every nurse that fit his description try it on for size.

The supervisor turned on her heel. "I'll have Stephanie assigned to your room for the day."

"Thank you."

After they left, Geoff lay back against the pillows and waited for Stephanie Brandt to appear.

With each passing moment, his heart thumped harder against the wall of his chest at the idea that he would be seeing his angel again. "Don't be a fool now," he muttered to himself.

"That's good advice for anytime, not just today," a soft voice said.

The voice was familiar and he knew that the supervisor had located his angel. No, not his angel. His nurse. Stephanie Brandt.

He turned and stared at her. She was just as beautiful as he remembered her. Last night he'd only gotten a glimpse of her. Now staring at her head-on, he realized that there were no words to describe her. *Stunning* and *gorgeous* were inadequate. He searched his mind for something intelligent to say, but words escaped him.

Stephanie stepped fully into the room, coming to stand beside his bed. "I understand that you requested me to be your nurse today."

He finally found his voice. "I did."

"Why?"

Suddenly he didn't have a reason. At least not one that he could share with her. He couldn't just blurt out that he'd felt a connection to her. Saying that might make her uncomfortable. They'd been around each other for fewer than ten minutes and he knew that it took more time than that to make a real connection. "You seemed to care about my welfare yesterday. And since the doctors are insisting that I spend the rest of the day and night here, I wanted a nurse I felt comfortable with."

"Any of the nurses here will treat you well. I didn't do anything special for you that anyone else wouldn't have done."

"You may be right, but seeing a familiar face should make my imprisonment here more palatable."

She laughed and warmth spread throughout his body. The sound was so happy and carefree. But more than that, it was authentic. She wasn't pretending to be amused by him in order to win his favor. "You're lying in a comfortable bed with clean sheets. You'll have your choice from several meal options, which will be brought to you. You have a television with an admittedly poor selection of programs for you to watch during your stay. And a telephone. I don't think this fits anyone's definition of prison by a long shot."

"Maybe not, but I'm not free to leave."

"For your own good."

"So you all say." He realized he was pouting and tried to stop acting like an infant. When did he become a baby-man?

"How's your arm feel?" Stephanie leaned over and checked his bandages. Her sweet scent wafted under his nose, and he closed his eyes in pleasure. Maybe he wasn't allowed to leave, but he no longer wanted to. At least not as long as she was around to keep him company.

"It's throbbing a bit, but nothing I can't handle." He didn't want to take any more painkillers and risk becoming loopy again. Who knew what would come out of his mouth then. Besides, he wanted to be alert and enjoy her company.

"Don't go all tough guy on me. If you need pain medication let me know. There's no need to suffer unnecessarily."

"I won't."

She checked his vitals and then made a notation on his chart.

"Is everything okay?" he asked her.

"Perfect. I'll be back in a little while to check on you."

"You're leaving?" He frowned. "They said you were going to be my nurse."

"And I am. But I'm not exclusively your nurse. I have several other patients that need my attention, too."

Geoff hadn't expected that and he reminded himself that there was nothing manly about acting like a spoiled brat.

"I'll do my rounds and come back to check on you as soon as I can. How's that sound?"

"That sounds good." Geoff waited until Stephanie was out of the room before crossing his fingers and wishing that he was her only patient. It was childish, he knew, but he'd take any luck he could get.

* * *

Stephanie walked out of Geoff Burris's room and once she was certain he could no longer see her, sagged against the wall. Inhaling deeply, she struggled to regain her equilibrium. Whew. That was not the way she'd expected to start her day. When she'd arrived at work for her shift, she'd been told by Doris, her supervisor, to report to a patient's room. It wasn't an entirely unusual order so she hadn't given it much thought. She'd been caught completely off guard when she'd walked in and seen Geoff Burris lying in the bed, the covers only reaching his waist. His chest was bare except for the bandages protecting his shoulder and biceps. It had taken Herculean effort to keep from drooling. Hopefully he hadn't been able to see how affected she'd been.

Stephanie couldn't believe that her proximity to Geoff Burris had changed her into something she never thought she'd be: a complete and total fangirl.

Stephanie stood upright and looked around, grateful that no one had noticed her momentary weakness. She was at work, for goodness' sake. Once more she reminded herself that Geoff had just undergone surgery. The last thing he needed was for his nurse to go all wonky on him. He needed professional care. Dispassionate care. Care that she ordinarily provided very easily but which was in short supply because of the way being around Geoff Burris affected her. Lucky for her, she would have other patients to care for, so she wouldn't be spending a lot of time with him.

Once she'd regained her self-control, Stephanie strode purposefully toward the nurses' station and checked the board where nurse-patient assignments were listed. She found her name and followed it down. No, that couldn't be right. There was only one patient assigned to her. Geoff Burris.

She scanned the hallway for Doris and walked down to her, quickly explaining how the board must be wrong.

Her supervisor stopped her mid-sentence. "The chart is correct. You only have one patient. Why, is he misbehaving?" Doris was protective of her nurses and wouldn't tolerate anyone mistreating them. She'd go to the mat for them and they would do the same for her.

"Nothing like that. He's actually been very nice. I just thought I'd have more patients."

"You can thank Dr. Wilson for that. He made the request."

"Why?"

"He's concerned that your patient might try and fly the coop. After meeting him myself, I'm inclined to agree. Since you always go above and beyond, and we only have a few patients today, I decided that you have earned an easy day."

"So he's my only patient?" Stephanie repeated although Doris had been perfectly clear.

"Yes. Is that going to be a problem? Because if it is I can assign someone else to his care despite the fact that he specifically asked for you."

Geoff Burris had requested her? Wow. She didn't quite know what to make of that. Foolish butterflies began floating through her stomach and she swatted them away. She wasn't going to turn into a silly schoolgirl over a simple request. "It's not going to be a problem. I just want to carry my fair share of the load."

"You always have. To be honest, I imagine our superstar is used to having his every wish granted, so you may end up doing more than your fair share today."

Stephanie didn't get that impression from Geoff. True, he was rich and famous, two qualities that generally went hand-in-hand with being demanding, but Geoff seemed humble and considerate. There hadn't been anything demanding about him. Heck, she'd encountered doctors who'd tried to get away with treating nurses as servants instead of valuable members of the team before they'd been set straight.

"I'll just get back to his room then and see if he's ordered his lunch yet."

Doris nodded and then walked away.

Before returning to Geoff's room, Stephanie

made a detour into the ladies' room and checked her makeup. As she retouched her lipstick, she called herself all kinds of foolish. He was her patient. The fact that he'd specifically asked for her didn't mean anything. She was the first nurse he'd met and like most people, he preferred the known to the unknown. As long as she remembered that she would be fine.

That decided, she ran a comb through her shoulder-length hair—not because she was trying to look good for Geoff, but rather because her hair had been whipped by the wind and she hadn't had a chance to put it in order before she'd started work. She frowned at her reflection. Even she didn't believe that lie.

Geoff's eyes were closed when she returned to his room. When she stepped inside, they opened and he smiled. "You came back."

She shrugged and tried to ignore the tingling sensation that raced up and down her spine at the pleasure in his voice. "It turns out that you're the only patient I'm assigned to today."

His smile broadened. He pushed the button controlling his bed, lifting the head until he was in a sitting position, once more giving her an unobstructed view of his sculpted chest and six-pack abs. Geoff was definitely a perfect specimen who looked out of place in a hospital bed.

He gestured to the chair beside his bed. "Have

a seat. If you're going to keep me company, I don't expect you to stand up for hours."

Stephanie looked at the chair and noted its proximity to the bed. Less than twelve inches separated them. Deciding it would look odd if she stood up the entire time, she sat down. Besides, she would be spending a lot of time in his room so she might as well make herself comfortable. "Thanks. I'll leave if you have any visitors."

"I'm not expecting anyone."

"Really? I thought you were from here."

"I am. I grew up in Bronco Valley."

"Your family isn't going to visit you?"

"They were here yesterday and before the surgery this morning. I sent them home because I thought I was going to be released today." He shot her an accusatory frown as though she were the one making him spend the night in the hospital. He looked so much like a disappointed little boy that she couldn't help but smile.

"Clearly you're not used to being inactive."

"No. I have a lot of things to do and I'm lying here in bed, not accomplishing a thing."

"That's not true. You're doing something very important."

"What? Amusing you?"

"No. Well, yes, but that's not what I was going to say. You're giving your body a chance to heal. You were badly injured yesterday."

"I've been hurt before. It goes with the territory."

That was a cavalier attitude to have toward one's body. "Did you require surgery?"

"No." His voice sounded begrudging.

"Well, then I'm guessing this injury was a little bit more serious than the others, so you need to recover a bit differently than you did before. Surely this can't be the worst place you've ever spent the night."

The frown fled and his eyes lit with mirth and he chuckled and her heart skipped a beat in response. "You've got me there. When I started, I didn't have much money so, yes, I've had worse accommodations than this."

"Tell me about your life on the road. What's it like?"

"Then or now?"

"Either. Both. We've got hours to fill."

He rubbed a hand over his chin for a moment as if deciding which story to tell. His jaw was covered with dark stubble. It looked good on him. "I'll start with when I first went on the circuit."

"How old were you?"

"Eighteen. My parents weren't enthused about my decision to not go to college, but after a while, they realized that trying to change my mind was futile. I was determined to join the rodeo."

"Did you ride before?"

"Yes. I started when I was about nine. At first

my parents thought it was just a passing fancy. I'd already done the whole Pop Warner football thing, played Little League baseball, and even basketball for a year or two. I'd enjoyed those sports well enough, but there was something about bronc riding that excited me in a way the other sports hadn't. It was in my blood. I stuck with it throughout high school. I won a few trophies over the years." He smiled and she had a feeling he was being modest. No doubt he'd won more than his share. For the first time she wished she'd paid more attention when her brothers talked about rodeo and Bronco's hometown hero.

"Anyway," he continued, "I joined the circuit shortly after high school graduation. At first I only competed in Montana and neighboring states on the weekend when my father could accompany me. We stayed in fleabag motels and ate at greasy spoons. I think he was trying to show me how hard and uncomfortable life in rodeo would be so I would change my mind and go to college. But I surprised him by sticking it out. Life on the road was often bad, but it was worth it. Eventually my parents accepted that I was going to make a career of rodeo."

She nodded as she imagined him the first time he had to sleep on a lumpy mattress in a cheap motel. Her admiration for him grew as she realized how committed he was to being in the rodeo even if it wasn't always comfortable.

"How did they react?"

"They bought me a reliable pickup truck and made me promise to keep in touch when I traveled alone. Of course our definition of 'keeping in touch' differed. They wanted me to check in every night before I went to bed. And of course they wanted to know where I was staying."

"That sounds reasonable."

He snorted.

"I'm serious. That sounds fair."

"Did you go away to college?"

"Yes."

"How old were you? Eighteen?"

She nodded.

"Did you stay in a dorm?"

She grinned. "I get where you're going with this. But there's a difference between living on campus with a residence hall director and traveling across the country on your own."

"I know it's not exactly the same thing. And I made a point to call my parents whenever I went to a new city. And I always let them know where I was staying. But checking in every night? No way."

"Didn't you ever get homesick?"

"Sure. I missed my parents and my brothers. I love them."

There was something about the way he spoke so easily about his feelings that warmed her heart. Family was important to her and she loved hers, too. "But you stayed on the road?"

"Yes. But then one after the other my brothers joined the circuit. We often compete in the same rodeos, so I get to spend time with them."

"What about your parents? How often do you see them?"

"Not as much as I would like. My dad is a high school principal and my mother is a kindergarten teacher, so they can't just drop everything and follow us around. For the past few years, I've been so busy on the tour and with other commitments that I haven't gotten home as often as I would like. And when I do, the visits are really quick. That's why I'm so excited about the Mistletoe Rodeo. It's a chance to merge both of my worlds. And I'm not even home a week before I end up lying in a stupid hospital bed."

"Hey, don't go insulting our beds."

He laughed as she'd hoped he would. She understood that people in pain often lashed out in frustration, but she could also tell that he was a good guy and she wanted to keep the mood light. "I imagine driving from place to place and staying in one dumpy hotel after another has to get old."

"It did. Although a lot of the rodeos are held in out-of-the-way places, there are often good hotels nearby. But now I have an RV. It's my home away from home. And I get to sleep in my own bed every night."

She nodded. Traveling in a motor home sounded better than the alternative, but she couldn't imagine living the vagabond life. She appreciated a good vacation as much as the next person and had traveled to Fiji a few years back with her sisters, Tiffany and Brittany, but she needed roots. She liked the comfort that came from familiar surroundings. There was something peaceful about getting her morning coffee at Bronco Java and Juice and shooting the breeze with her regular barista. And she enjoyed having Sunday dinners at her parents' house, joking with her brothers, Ethan and Lucas, and chatting with her sisters. She liked knowing her family was nearby.

"I talked about myself enough. What about you?"

"What about me?" There was nothing special about her life. When she'd left home at eighteen, it had been to attend college to become a nurse, a dream she'd had since she was eleven. She'd spent most of her time studying in the library. The most exciting thing she'd done was join a sorority. But even then, there was nothing wild about her or her sorority sisters. They were part of the Divine Nine who were serious about community service. After graduation she'd returned home. Nothing in her experience could compare to the life he'd lived.

"Tell me about your family. Your life. Where your boyfriend takes you on dates."

"Is that your clever way of asking me if I have a boyfriend?"

His grin was rueful and simultaneously charming. "Evidently not as clever as I thought."

"I'm not dating anyone currently." That was an understatement, but he didn't need to know the sorry state of her romantic life. She had an up-and-down dating history. There would be months when it seemed as if someone had draped an invisibility cloak over her. Then there were other times when men vied for her attention. Sadly, the most recent months fell into the former category.

"Okay. Well, tell me about your family. I always feel at a disadvantage meeting new people. The media have followed me for years, reporting on every little thing that I do, so I have very few secrets. Other people always know so much more about me than I know about them."

"Well, if it's any consolation, I'm not a big fan of rodeo and don't follow you at all, so I know very little about you. I'm sure you have plenty of secrets from me."

"I don't know whether to feel insulted that you aren't a fan of my life's work or relieved that you don't know everything about me."

"Why not both?"

Geoff laughed and she joined him. "Why not both indeed. But still, I told you about myself, so tell me about your life."

"Okay. I'm one of five children. I have two sisters and two brothers. My parents own a dry-cleaning business with numerous locations across the state. They spent a lot of time building the business when my siblings and I were growing up, so we were raised to be responsible and self-sufficient. They taught us to take care of ourselves as well as each other."

He nodded. "My parents raised us the same way."

"My older sister, Brittany, got married recently to a man who is raising his infant niece." Stephanie grinned as she recalled her sister bringing home Daniel Dubois and his baby niece Hailey to meet the family. Daniel had gotten custody of Hailey after her parents had been killed in a car crash and was raising her as his daughter. "She was initially his event planner, but they fell in love really quickly and got married, surprising us all."

"Why was it a surprise?"

"Brittany was always focused on her career. Plus she always swore she didn't want kids. Even though we all had responsibilities at home, Brittany was the oldest so she always felt like she had to look out for the rest of us. Then she meets a man with a baby and gets married within weeks. That definitely didn't sound like the sister I grew up with. But she's happier than I've ever seen her so obviously it was the right thing for her to do."

"That's all that matters."

"Yes. But her life changed in the blink of an eye. I guess that's how love works."

"For some. I can't see changing my whole life just because I met a woman. No matter how great she is. Rodeo and permanent relationships don't mix. I'm not ready to give up rodeo so…"

Stephanie made a mental note even though it wasn't necessary. She and Geoff weren't dating and she certainly wasn't contemplating a future with him. She was his nurse and was keeping him company because she'd been assigned the task. If he'd met a different nurse last night, she would be in here instead of Stephanie, and Geoff would be having this conversation with *her*.

The food service worker knocked on the open door and brought in Geoff's lunch. Stephanie stepped out of the way while the young man placed the tray on the wheeled table and then moved the table over to Geoff.

Geoff looked at the food and smiled. "Thank you."

"You're welcome." The guy just stood there, staring at Geoff.

"Is there something else?" Stephanie asked when the worker didn't leave.

"I was wondering if I came back after I got off work, would you take a picture with me to show my parents and friends? We're all big fans."

"No," Stephanie said at the same time that Geoff said, "Sure."

Both men turned to stare at her. Geoff looked surprised. The worker looked nervous. He'd stepped over the line and he knew it.

"I don't mind taking a picture," Geoff said.

"You're supposed to be resting and recovering."

Geoff looked back at the employee. "What's your name?"

"Billy."

"What time do you get off, Billy?"

"In an hour."

"Come back then and we'll take that picture."

"Thanks." Billy scurried from the room before Stephanie could say anything to him. Hospital policy was clear. Patients shouldn't be hassled. Their privacy needed to be respected. True, they didn't have famous patients often, but the rule still applied.

"You're here to rest," Stephanie said.

"I'm just going to take a picture. What's the worst that could happen?"

Stephanie raised an eyebrow. "How did you end up in that bed?"

He barked out a laugh and silly little tingles danced down Stephanie's spine until they reached her toes. Down, girl. "Touché. I should have said nothing else can happen. Besides I won't be standing on bleachers. I'll be lying in bed. I can't get into too much trouble that way. At least not alone."

Was he flirting with her? Of course not. He probably didn't realize that his words had the power to make her shiver. And truly they shouldn't have. "I'm going to let you eat while I grab some food of my own."

"You can bring it back and eat with me if you want. And if it looks appetizing, you might have mercy on a poor soul like me and share."

She laughed. "I'm not sure my lunch is any better than yours. I'm having a salad and a bowl of soup."

"Oh. In that case I'll take pity on you and share my lunch with you. At least I have green Jell-O."

"I'll be back in a little while."

"Okay."

Stephanie left the room and darted to the nurses' lounge. She was grabbing her lunch box from the fridge when Lisa, another nurse, stepped inside. Lisa had set her sights on Dr. Williamson, a handsome and charming young doctor who'd recently joined the medical staff. Although Stephanie had a rule against dating coworkers, she wasn't opposed to being friends with him and they had the occasional coffee together. Stephanie had told Lisa more than once that she had no designs on the man, but either it hadn't sunk in or Lisa didn't believe her. Lisa had decided that Stephanie was her competition for the doctor's affection and therefore she and Stephanie couldn't be friends.

Stephanie pulled the glass container of soup from the bag and placed it in the microwave.

"Hi," Lisa said cheerfully.

Stephanie looked around, half expecting to see someone entering the room, but there was no one else. Apparently Lisa was talking to her.

"Hi," Stephanie said, then turned to look back at the microwave, watching the bowl spin slowly.

"So, you're taking care of our VIP patient."

Ah. No wonder Lisa was being so friendly. She probably wanted an introduction. "Where did you hear that?"

"Word gets around. If he needs someone to sit with him while you eat, I'm willing to give up my lunch to do it. I'm not all that hungry. Besides, I'm a big fan."

Did this mean Lisa was no longer interested in Dr. Williamson? Apparently any rich man would do. There might not be a snowball's chance that anything would happen between Stephanie and Geoff, but there was no way she was going to leave him at the mercy of this barracuda. Stephanie looked at Lisa, her smile just as fake as Lisa's. "Thanks, but he requested me. We're going to eat lunch together in his room."

Lisa's smile faded. Ah, the end of a beautiful friendship.

The microwave dinged and Stephanie removed the bowl, grabbed her salad and then returned to Geoff's room. She hadn't intended to eat with him, but she'd boxed herself in a corner with a lie. So much for time to regroup.

The rest of the afternoon passed pleasantly and she had to admit that she enjoyed spending her shift with Geoff. He was fun and charming and not the least bit stuck on himself. Sure he was a big star, but he didn't behave as if the world revolved around him or as if other people only existed to serve him and stroke his ego. Geoff took three selfies with Billy and autographed multiple pieces of paper for friends and family. Stephanie might not have agreed with Geoff's decision, but she had to admit that Billy was positively beaming when he left the room.

Geoff nodded off occasionally during the afternoon, taking a few brief naps. Stephanie administered his medication and took his vitals a few times during the day and she was pleased that they were within normal range. Now, hours later, he was staring at her with slightly glassy eyes. No doubt he would sleep well tonight. If everything remained the same, he would be released some-time tomorrow morning.

She glanced at her watch and then stood. "Well, that's it for me. My shift is over." Actually it had ended thirty minutes ago.

His eyes widened. "You're leaving?"

"Yes."

Tomorrow was her day off. It hit her then that she wouldn't be seeing Geoff again. When she re-turned to work, he'd already have been released. They didn't run in the same circles so there was no chance of her bumping into him at a friend's house. Besides, he needed to stay home and recu-perate, not gallivant around Bronco. "Good luck with the rodeo."

"So that's it? You're just going to walk out of my life?"

"Yep." She flashed him a saucy grin to cover the strange ache in her heart. It didn't make sense for her to feel bereft when she'd only met the man last night. He was a patient, not a friend, no mat-ter how comfortable she felt with him.

"If you're leaving, then I guess I'll do the same." He grabbed his blankets and tossed them aside.

"What are you talking about? You haven't been released yet. You have to stay until tomorrow morning." Stephanie heard the panic in her voice, but she couldn't help it. She didn't want Geoff to do more damage to his arm. And he'd sprained his ankle, so she didn't know how he intended to stand, much less walk. But over the past hours she'd learned that he was determined, so she had no doubt he'd find a way.

"I'll stay under one condition."

"What's that?" She knew she shouldn't negotiate with him, but she was desperate.

"You have dinner with me when I'm released."

"You're saying you're going to check out against medical advice if I don't go on a date with you."

"Not just a date. Dinner. And yes, I mean it, Stephanie."

Stephanie didn't believe for a minute that Geoff was serious. More than likely his latest dose of painkillers was doing the talking. But since she didn't want to risk his health, she decided to humor him. After a good night's sleep, he would more than likely forget all about this conversation. Or if he did recall it, he would probably try to find a way to wiggle out of the agreement.

"Well?" he said while she stood there having a conversation with herself.

"Yes. I'll go to dinner with you if you stay in the hospital."

"Good." He leaned back against the pillows and covered himself with the blankets. They were crooked and she automatically straightened them. Doing so required her to lean over him. The heat from his body wrapped around her and Stephanie had to bite her bottom lip to keep a groan from escaping. She pulled back and their eyes met. Mere inches separated them. Electricity arced between them, freezing her in place.

A loud noise in the hallway broke the spell and she jumped. Standing, she mentally chastised herself. What in the world was she doing? Geoff Burris was a patient. She was behaving as inappropriately as Billy had earlier. In fact, her transgression was even further over the line.

She cleared her throat and forced herself to look back at Geoff. He was staring at her, his eyes dark and unreadable. "Do you need anything else before I go?"

"No." His voice was husky. Hoarse.

"The night nurse will be in to check on you later. Naturally you can ring for her if you need anything." She realized she was on the verge of babbling and pressed her lips together.

"I won't."

"Good night, then."

"Good night. See you soon."

Stephanie stepped outside his room, partially closing his door behind her. Then she went to the locker room where she changed clothes, put on her coat and raced from the hospital as if the devil himself were on her heels, not slowing until she was safely ensconced in her car. She didn't know what had just happened between her and Geoff, but she had a feeling Winona Cobbs's words were truer now than they were yesterday.

Stephanie could run, but she couldn't hide from the truth. The rodeo star was perilously close to lassoing her, after all.

Chapter Three

"For someone who claims to be in a hurry to get out of this place, you sure are taking your sweet time." Mike groaned. Ever since he'd arrived at the hospital forty minutes ago, he'd been sprawled in the guest chair and scrolling on his phone. After helping himself to Geoff's breakfast.

Geoff looked up from shoving his foot into the one boot that he could wear and stared at his younger brother who smirked at him. Geoff had convinced his parents to let Mike pick him up so neither of them would have to take off from work. They were needed at school. Besides, Geoff knew his mother would hover over him, something his brother would never do. Right now Geoff was re-thinking the wisdom of that decision. He'd forgotten how annoying Mike could be.

"Didn't you hear the nurse say there was a page missing from my post-op instructions?"

"I did. But still, I would think you'd have your boots on by now. Or rather boot. It looks to me like you've lowered the anchor, slowing things down."

"Why would I do that?" Geoff asked as if it were the most ridiculous thing he'd ever heard, trying to throw his brother off the scent before Mike realized just how right he was. Geoff had been hoping Stephanie would show up before he left. She knew that he was being released today. Even if she had been assigned to other patients, she could stop in to say hello. So far she hadn't.

He knew his disappointment was outsized and even a bit entitled. He and Stephanie weren't friends and she was under no obligation to visit him. But he'd felt a very real connection to her and believed that she felt the same. There was that one moment last night before she'd left that they'd come close to kissing. But that noise had ruined the moment and she'd run from the room like her shoes were on fire.

But maybe the interest had been one-sided. After all, Stephanie had said that any other nurse would have treated him the same way as she had. To her way of thinking, he and any other nurse would have gotten along just as well. Geoff didn't believe that for a minute. He'd never been as comfortable with another woman as he'd felt with Stephanie. And he certainly hadn't told anyone else some of the things he'd shared with her.

Mike gave him a knowing look. "I don't know. Maybe you're waiting for someone to stop in and see you?"

Geoff jerked and pain immediately shot through his arm. He really needed to stop doing that. "Who would I be waiting to see?"

"That's twice you answered a question with a question when I was just making an observation. Maybe I'm onto something. You're moving slowly because you're waiting for someone. Am I right?"

"What you are is annoying."

Mike threw back his head and laughed. He was too smart for his own good. "I can't believe you made a conquest while you were stuck in the hospital."

"She's not a conquest so don't call her that."

"Sorry. But instead of waiting around for this non-conquest to arrive, why don't you just go find her."

"Go find who?" asked the nurse who stepped into the room. Annie, a middle-aged woman who moved at the speed of light, looked from Mike to Geoff. "Let me help you with that," she said, taking his unused boot and placing it into a clear plastic bag with the hospital's name printed on it.

"Thanks."

"I have your discharge papers as well as a prescription for pain medication. You can have it filled at any pharmacy."

Geoff took the papers and shoved them into the plastic bag beside his boot.

"Who are you looking for?" Annie asked again

as she helped him into the wheelchair. He'd spent enough time in hospitals to know they took wheeling the patient to the front door very seriously. Over the years he'd tried to charm and cajole and wheedle his way around that requirement but had never once succeeded.

"My nurse from yesterday. Stephanie Brandt. I was hoping to thank her for her wonderful care before I left."

The nurse turned shrewd eyes on him before answering. First Mike and now this nurse. Geoff must be as transparent as this bag. "Stephanie isn't scheduled to work today. I'll be sure to relay your appreciation to her."

Geoff managed to squelch his disappointed sigh before it could escape. Why was he upset that Stephanie wasn't working today? Everyone deserved a day off and this happened to be hers. So why hadn't she told him this last night? Apparently she didn't care enough about his feelings to tell him. Or maybe she thought he didn't need to know. He knew he was making a mountain out of a molehill as his mother would say, but he couldn't help himself. Perhaps it was the medication still flowing through his veins that had him thinking so irrationally. That was the only explanation he could think of.

"I'll go get the car," Mike said.

Geoff scanned the room to be sure that he

wasn't leaving anything behind. Not that he'd had all that much to begin with. His brother, Ross, had taken his broken phone and promised to get Geoff a replacement. What remained of the pullover he'd worn to the photo shoot was inside the plastic bag on his lap. Mike had brought him a flannel button-down shirt from home that Geoff had struggled to put on over his surgically repaired arm. Annie had offered her assistance, but Geoff had refused. The only nurse he wanted touching him wasn't on duty today.

"Let's get moving," Annie said, rescuing Geoff before he could throw himself a pity party. He put his feet onto the footrests and Annie wheeled him from the room. While they were waiting for the elevator, a little boy of about six ran over, held up his arm which was covered in a light blue cast, and asked Geoff to sign it.

"My mom and dad are taking me to see you ride at the Mistletoe Rodeo," the kid said as Geoff scrawled his name with a black marker. "I'm going to make a poster and cheer for you."

"I'll look for that poster and listen for your voice."

"I can yell really loud. Do you want to hear?" The boy inhaled and his skinny chest expanded.

"You probably shouldn't yell in the hospital," Geoff said, pointing at Annie. "The nurses might not like it."

"Oh, yeah. I forgot."

The elevator came, and Annie spun the wheelchair around and backed Geoff inside. When they reached the lobby, he was happy to see Mike's pickup truck outside. Though his brother jumped out of the truck to help him, Annie insisted on getting him in the vehicle.

Mike hopped into the driver's side with ease. "Ready?"

Geoff snorted. "I've been ready since the moment they brought me here."

Mike pulled out of the circular driveway and onto the road. At this time of day, traffic was light. As they drove down the main street, Geoff looked around. He hadn't had much time to wander around town before he'd gotten hurt. He'd been too busy speaking with his agent as they finalized the deal to represent Taylor Beef.

Now, he looked at the shops lining the street and wondered which places Stephanie frequented. Did she get her morning cup of coffee at Bronco Java and Juice or grab a sandwich at the nearby deli? Or did she prefer to dine at DJ's Deluxe? Did she hang out with friends at Wild Willa's Saloon?

He frowned and shook his head. Why was he thinking about Stephanie? She certainly wasn't wasting a moment thinking about him. To her, he'd simply been one more patient. Sure, she'd appeared to have a good time with him, but what else

could she do? She'd been assigned to his case—
at his request. It wasn't as if she'd sought him out
to hang out with him. She'd been paid to spend
time with him.

"What's wrong?" Mike asked, breaking into
Geoff's thoughts. And not a moment too soon.
"Why are you frowning? Are you in pain? If you
want, I can fill your prescription for you before
we go home."

"I'm fine. I was just thinking about something."

"Well, it must have been something horrible to
make you look like that."

"It's nothing."

Mike nodded, but Geoff knew he hadn't convinced his brother. But he also knew Mike
wouldn't press him to talk.

Although Geoff was the oldest and had always
tried to set a good example for his younger brothers while they were growing up, and often had
to play the role of the tough big brother to keep
them in line, over the years they had become
good friends. Trusted friends. At twenty-three,
Mike was the youngest, with Ross and Jack being
twenty-four and twenty-seven respectively. They
had different personalities and life goals, but they
shared values and perspectives and the ability to
understand each other without words.

When Mike reached their parents' home, he
pulled into the driveway. Ross and Jack immedi-

ately emerged from the house and were down the stairs before Geoff was out of the truck. The concern on their faces warmed his heart and his vision blurred for the briefest moment.

"Big brother," Ross said, rushing over to Geoff, his arms outstretched as if to give him a huge hug. Geoff braced himself for the pain he knew was coming. At the last second, Ross stopped, a mischievous grin on his face. "Just kidding."

"You play too much," Jack said, but he was laughing as he turned to Geoff, holding out a crutch. "You need help walking?"

"Nah. I got it," Geoff said, taking the crutch and leaning on it with his good arm. Growing up, Geoff and his brothers had sprained enough ankles and twisted enough knees that their parents had an assortment of medical supplies on hand.

"It's been a while since I've had to use one of these," he said as he limped up the stairs, his brothers close enough to catch him if he should stumble. By the time he was standing on the porch he was breathing hard, but he refused to take a break until he'd made it into the living room. He grabbed the back of his father's favorite brown leather recliner and inhaled deeply. He couldn't take another step. If it was this hard to simply walk, he was going to have a heck of a time staying on the back of a bucking bronco. He needed to get the remainder of the pain medicine out of his system fast so he wouldn't be so sluggish.

Once he'd caught his breath, he slowly removed his jacket and draped it over the back of the chair. His mother had always insisted that they hang their coats in the hall closet the minute they stepped into the house, but he'd just had surgery and was exhausted. Besides, she wasn't here to see. He'd hang it up as soon as he got his second wind. He slumped onto the sofa, grabbed a pillow and set it on the coffee table and gingerly placed his injured foot there. All at once, he wished his mother was around to pamper him. He'd be lucky if one of his brothers brought him a glass of water. It wasn't as if they didn't care about him. That just wasn't the way guys thought.

Jack grabbed the remote and then sat at the other end of the sofa. He was big into nature and watched documentaries whenever he had the chance.

"I'm going to run out to the pharmacy and get your medicine," Mike said. "I'll be back in a few."

"Save yourself the trouble. That stuff makes me loopy." And it wreaked havoc on his emotions. How else could he explain his ridiculous reaction to not seeing Stephanie today? And speaking of Stephanie, why hadn't he gotten her telephone number? He would love to hear her soothing voice right about now. "I'm not taking anything stronger than an aspirin."

"Are you nuts? You just had surgery. You might not be in a lot of pain now, but that's probably because there's still residual medicine in your system. Trust me, when it wears off, you're going to be begging for this medicine. The doctor wouldn't have prescribed it if you didn't need it."

Geoff waited for his other brothers to chime in and show their support for Geoff, but they didn't. Instead, Ross nodded in agreement and Jack kept his eyes glued to the television even though a beer commercial they'd all seen a hundred times was playing. Geoff sighed. Everyone knew that Mike was starting medical school next year and that he'd saved most of his earnings for tuition. Although he enjoyed rodeo, it wasn't his dream. Geoff still didn't understand how Mike had managed to graduate from college while competing on the circuit, but he'd pulled it off.

After Geoff had begun getting sponsors who paid an outrageous amount of money for him to represent their products, Geoff had offered to pay for Mike's education, but his brother had turned him down flat, insisting that he could and would pay his own way. Mike definitely had a double dose of the Burris pride. Geoff respected his brother's independence, but even so, unbeknownst to his youngest brother, Geoff had set aside a substantial amount of money to help him pay for medical school. Family helped family.

"Suit yourself," Geoff grumbled and closed his eyes, putting an end to that conversation. When he opened his eyes, the television was off and he was alone. A blanket had been thrown over him and a pillow had been placed behind his head. Maybe his brothers weren't that bad after all.

He stretched as much as his surgically repaired arm would allow and then sat up and looked around. The sun was no longer streaming through the front windows although it hadn't set yet. His stomach growled and he realized he hadn't eaten in hours. Inhaling, he got a whiff of delicious food.

"I thought you'd be awake by now," his mother said as she came into the room, carrying a tray. As she drew closer, he realized there was a plate of the chicken and dumplings he'd asked her to cook yesterday.

"What time is it?"

"Almost four thirty."

"Four thirty?" He'd been asleep for hours. "I slept most of the day away."

"Did you have someplace to go?" his mother said in the tone that only mothers could get away with using. It wasn't quite snark or sarcasm, but it came close enough to touch.

"I guess not."

"Didn't think so. Go wash your hands so you

can eat. Then we'll talk about leaving your clothes all over the house as if you were a snake shedding skin."

He gave her a look and she laughed and helped him stand. He made a quick trip to the bathroom and when he returned his mother had added a saucer containing a slice of caramel pound cake to the tray. He guessed that meant all was forgiven.

He dug into his food. After one bite he let out a long sigh. Delicious. Absolutely nothing in the world tasted as good as his mother's food. Even though he now could afford to eat at the best restaurants in every town he traveled to, and did on occasion, he would choose his mother's home cooking if given the chance. His father had always joked that her food tasted so good because of her secret ingredient—love. Geoff was inclined to agree. It was going to be great to feast on her cooking before he had to hit the road again.

His mother returned, a mug of hot chocolate in her hand. She sat down in her favorite chair and then blew over the beverage before taking a sip.

"You know you don't have to wait on me hand and foot, right?" he asked her. Then before she could respond, he added, "But I appreciate it." Which earned a smile.

"How was work?" Geoff asked as he dug into his meal.

Jeanne's eyes lit up. "Wonderful. I do believe

this class is the sweetest and smartest that I've ever had."

Geoff laughed. She said that every year. The kids who'd had his mother as a teacher were the luckiest in town. Jeanne loved kids and made sure that her students got her best effort every day. On more than one occasion, she'd asked him to send signed photos to her kids as rewards for doing well. He'd even visited her school a couple of times and spoken at assemblies. He didn't much like public speaking, but he enjoyed spending time with the children. But her devotion wasn't limited to her pupils. She made a point to get to know their parents and siblings. Jeanne was often the first person to know about struggles her families faced and the first to offer help.

"And how are things with you?" his mother asked. "Anything new?"

"What do you mean?" Geoff asked, wondering what she was getting at.

His mother somehow knew all. But then, she'd taught kindergarten for over thirty years. She was beloved by former students as well as their families who worked in industries all across the city if not the state. Maybe even the country. She had a network of spies the CIA would envy.

She raised a perfectly shaped eyebrow as she lifted the cup to her lips. Yep. She knew about Stephanie. The question was how much she knew.

He didn't want to volunteer information unnecessarily. His mother hadn't made a secret of the fact
that she wanted him to settle down and have a family. She never nagged, but over time her hints had
grown more direct. If he didn't act soon enough to
satisfy her, she would no doubt take matters into
her own hands. Heaven help him if she did.

She smiled as if deciding whether or not she
was going to play along. "I hear that you requested
a particular nurse to handle your care. Why was
that? Is this someone that you know from before?"

Before and after. That was how his mother
looked at his life. The "before" time lasted until
he joined the rodeo circuit and the "after" time
included everything since. He knew she liked the
people he'd known *before* more than those he'd met
after. Not that she would ever mistreat anyone. His
mother was much too loving and gracious for that.

Even knowing his mother's definition, he was
uncertain how to answer that question. He hadn't
known Stephanie before, but he hadn't met her on
the road, either. But then since she was a nurse his
mother would know that.

"No. I met Stephanie the day of the accident.
She was the nurse who took care of me initially.
And since I was forced to stay in the hospital yesterday," he said before reminding himself to stop
complaining about the past, "I requested that she
be assigned to me. After all, I'd already met her.

She didn't seem like the type of woman who would be interested in me simply because of my fame."

"That makes sense." She nodded and didn't say anything further. As a kid he'd often fallen into the trap of filling his mother's silence with conversation, which generally included a confession or details he'd wanted to hide.

"I thought so," he added when the silence had stretched on longer than he could stand. Apparently, despite the fact that none of her sons had lived here full-time for years, she hadn't lost her touch. "And it was nice spending the day with her."

She gave him a victorious grin. Little did she know that he'd held out on her.

"So are you taking Stephanie on a date?"

Geoff laughed. Maybe he wasn't as clever as he wanted to believe. "Yes. If that's all right with you." He smirked.

Jeanne grinned. "Don't be a smart aleck. You know I want you to meet a nice girl here in Bronco. That way, you'll be more inclined to come back for visits more often and maybe even settle down."

Settling down was out of the question. He was only going on one date with Stephanie, not starting a relationship.

Really? Was that the story he was going with? Because if that was the case, why had he been so determined to get her to agree to go to dinner with him? He didn't know the answer to that and he wasn't inclined to figure it out now. His shoulder and ankle were causing him enough pain. He didn't need to add a headache to the mix.

As if on cue, his shoulder and ankle began to throb and he groaned.

"Ready for your medicine?" his mother asked, rising.

"Yes." He was grateful that Mike insisted on filling the prescription for him so he wouldn't have to suffer for one more minute. Having a pesky little brother had its occasional benefit.

Jeanne went into the kitchen and came back with a pill bottle and a glass of water. She opened the bottle and tapped a capsule into Geoff's palm. He swallowed the pill and then leaned back against the sofa. His comfortable bed was calling, but he wanted to talk to his father tonight.

"Your father is coaching a basketball game tonight and then he's taking the team out for pizza," his mother said, reminding him of all the times she claimed that she could read his mind. "Why don't you go to bed now? He'll wake you when he gets home."

"Okay." Geoff grabbed his plate.

"I'll take care of your dishes. This time." His mother winked at him.

"Thanks."

It took monumental effort, but he made his way to his room. Getting out of his clothes and into a pair of pajama bottoms exhausted him. He climbed into bed and closed his eyes. He thought he would fall asleep immediately, but instead he found himself thinking of Stephanie and their upcoming date.

He couldn't wait.

Chapter Four

Stephanie was working on her charts at the nurses' station, listening with half an ear as two nurses discussed a patient's care with the chief resident, when the bouquet was delivered. Glancing at the beautiful arrangement of red roses, carnations and lilies with sprays of baby's breath, she sighed, wondering who the lucky recipient was. There were several patients on the ward today and the flowers could be for any one of them. But the arrangement was more romantic than those generally sent to someone who was recuperating. Of course, the flowers also could be for one of the doctors or nurses working today.

She looked at the messenger. "Those are gorgeous. Who are they for?"

He looked at his clipboard. "Stephanie Brandt."

Her heart leaped. "That's me."

"Would you sign for them?"

"Oh, yes." Smiling, she signed on the line indicated. "Thank you."

"Enjoy," the messenger said as he walked away.

"Oh, these are gorgeous," Tamara said, coming to stand beside Stephanie. "Who are they from?"

"I don't know," Stephanie said honestly.

"Is there a card?"

"Yes." Stephanie grabbed the small white envelope. Appreciative patients frequently sent thank-you cards and the occasional box of candy to the nurses. She briefly thought that the flowers could be from Geoff, but she immediately shot down that notion. She hadn't heard a peep out of him since she'd cared for him three days ago. Not that she'd expected to. Sure, he'd talked about taking her to dinner, and a small part of her heart had hoped that he'd meant it, but her brain had known better. Celebrities might date nurses in romantic comedies, but in the real world? Not so much. Besides, he'd been on strong painkillers at the time and probably had no recollection of extending the invitation.

She opened the envelope and then pulled out the card. She read the words written there and her heart skipped a beat. *For my angel.* Geoff's name was scrawled in the bold, confident signature that she recognized from the autographs he'd signed the other day.

"Who sent them?" Tamara asked as Stephanie stood there staring at the card, mesmerized.

Stephanie looked around at the growing crowd. Where there had only been a few other people around before, just about every nurse and several doctors had gathered. Did flowers generally garner this much attention? Honestly, yes, they did. Whenever one of the single women or heck, one of the single men received flowers or some other gift, it was big news that was expected to be shared with curious coworkers. Anything to lessen the stress of caring for seriously ill patients. But none of those flowers had ever been sent by a celebrity before. "Uh. Geoff Burris."

"Wow. You must have made quite an impression on him," Tamara said, winking.

"It wasn't like that," Stephanie protested. "The flowers are to show his appreciation. That's all."

"Then why are you blushing?"

Stephanie clapped her palms against her suddenly hot cheeks. "I'm not. I—I... Don't you people have work to do?"

Everyone laughed, but they did walk away, giving Stephanie some space. She tried to concentrate on the chart, but the floral scent kept teasing her, calling to her with its song, and she kept glancing at the flowers. Although she'd said that the bouquet was simply Geoff's way of thanking her, her foolish heart hoped that the flowers meant more than that. Once again she recalled the way that he'd pressed her to agree to have dinner with him. Could he have been serious? If he had been, why hadn't he contacted her before now?

Realizing that she wasn't going to be able to focus as long as she kept looking at the flowers, she grabbed her charts and went to check on her patients. She had administered medication and taken vitals not more than forty minutes ago, but it wouldn't hurt to give her patients a little more attention. It might do them a world of good to see a friendly face and be assured that she truly cared about their well-being.

Being in the hospital could be lonely and scary no matter a patient's age. The vulnerability that came with being unwell was often overwhelming.

Stephanie glanced in Mr. Harrison's room. He'd had his gallbladder removed a day ago and had been complaining about the blandness of hospital food earlier. Smiling brightly, she stepped inside. "How are you doing?"

"Ready to get out of here and back home where I can get some decent food. The cooks here don't know what seasoning is. And everything is boiled or broiled." He frowned at his lunch of skinless chicken breast and potatoes.

"If you'd rather have baked fish, I can have a new tray sent up to you."

"That's not any better. I couldn't convince you to run out and get me a nice, big steak and a side of fries, could I?"

She couldn't tell if he was serious or not. "No. Sorry."

"Didn't think so. Maybe I'll have better luck with my son."

Stephanie made a mental note to have a conversation with his son when he arrived later to let him know about the doctor's orders regarding his father's post-surgical diet. "You never know. See you later. Remember, use the call button if you need anything."

"I already requested a steak, but since you aren't inclined to give me that, I don't have much use for you." He smiled and winked so Stephanie knew he was joking.

She waved as she left to check on her other patients.

When she'd spoken with the others, she returned to the front desk, confident that she would be able to focus. She'd been there five minutes when an unnatural hush filled the air. Her nerve endings went on high alert. She didn't need to look around to know what had happened.

Geoff Burris had entered the ward.

Stephanie turned around. Geoff had stepped off the elevator and was striding across the floor, his eyes riveted to hers. She wanted to look away, but for the life of her she couldn't find the strength. His ankle must have healed because he wasn't using a crutch. His arm was still in a sling, though, but it didn't appear to be causing him any undue pain.

When he reached her, he smiled and gestured to the floral arrangement. "I see the flowers arrived."

"Yes. Thank you."

"Do you like them?"

"They're the most beautiful flowers I've ever seen."

"I'm glad you like them."

"And they're totally unnecessary."

"Not everything has to be needed. Sometimes a person can give a gift simply because he wants to."

She smiled, unsure what else to say. Suddenly aware that they had attracted an audience, she nodded her head to a family waiting area at the far side of the hall. "Let's talk in there."

"Sure."

"I'm taking a break," Stephanie said to everyone and no one in particular.

She took slow steps as she led Geoff to the area. They were the only people there and they sat in two chairs in front of the wide windows with an unobstructed view of the parking lot. It wasn't the most scenic spot, but it gave them a measure of privacy. Besides, they weren't going to have a romantic conversation. They were simply going to talk—about what she had no idea.

"How are you feeling?" she asked.

"I've felt better, but all things considered, I have no complaints. I just had a follow-up visit with Dr.

Wilson and he said I'm healing right on schedule. Whatever that means."

Her heart sank a little as she realized that Geoff hadn't made a special trip to see her. Of course he hadn't. Why would he? They weren't friends and they certainly weren't lovers. "That's good."

"The other reason I stopped by is to remind you of our date. When I got home, I realized that I hadn't gotten your phone number. I know it's possible to find just about anything on the internet, but I didn't want to do anything stalkerish, you know."

She laughed. "I appreciate your discretion."

"But then since I already knew that you worked at the hospital, I figured it would be okay to seek you out here to firm up the plans for our dinner."

"You don't have to do that. I have no intention of holding you to that date. I know that you were taking painkillers and how it can affect someone."

"I'm not sure what you mean by not holding me to that date. I'm the one who asked you out. Remember? And sure, I was in pain and a bit drugged, but I knew exactly what I was saying and doing. I want to go out with you. And you said that you would. Now the question is, did you only say yes because you felt pressure, or did you say yes because you want to go to dinner with me?"

Wow. Talk about being direct and getting straight to the point. Not that Stephanie was surprised. She'd spent an entire day with him. Although he'd slept on and off, they'd still done a lot of talking. In that time she'd discovered that he was a very straightforward person. He didn't beat around the bush or drop hints.

She took a deep breath and then looked around the room, stalling for time. Stephanie was a direct person herself, but she was more cautious when it came to affairs of the heart. She wasn't one for playing games, but she didn't go around blabbing about her feelings, either. At least not before she knew how the other person felt.

But then, they weren't about to embark on a romantic journey. She didn't know how often she needed to remind herself of that fact before it sank in. Geoff was only going to be in town for a short time. Then he was returning to his regularly scheduled life on the road. There was no chance that they could become emotionally involved in a few short weeks, so she wasn't vulnerable to heartbreak. With nothing to lose, she may as well throw caution to the wind.

Looking back at him, she smiled. "I would love to go out to dinner with you. When did you have in mind?"

"When is your next day off?"

"Tomorrow."

"How about tomorrow night, then? Or do you have other plans?"

"Tomorrow is fine."

"Great. I'll make reservations. Give me your address so I can pick you up."

Stephanie quickly told Geoff where she lived. After they agreed on the time, they stood. "I need to get back to work. See you tomorrow night."

He took her hand into his and then brushed his lips across the back of it. The kiss was feather soft, but it rocked her world. Her knees wobbled and she had to concentrate to stand upright. The last thing she wanted to do was sink to the floor at his feet. He smiled. "Until tomorrow."

"Tomorrow," she echoed, then turned and walked back to the nurses' station. Although she managed to maintain a calm facade, inside she was doing the happy dance. She had a date with Geoff Burris tomorrow night!

Her coworkers peppered her with questions the minute she stepped up to the desk. Uncomfortable being the subject of gossip, she didn't go into great detail. She simply said that Geoff had had a follow-up appointment with his doctor that day. He'd stopped by to see how she liked the flowers. Which was true. It just didn't include everything that had transpired.

The rest of the day seemed to crawl by, but finally her shift ended and she rushed home, eager to talk with her sisters. As the day had progressed, more and more of her coworkers had asked her questions about Geoff. Now she was beginning to wonder if she'd made a mistake by agreeing to go out with him. If receiving flowers from him created this much of a circus, what would happen if they were spotted together?

She made a quick sandwich and then phoned her sisters, Brittany and Tiffany. They talked often or got together when their schedules allowed. Now that Brittany was married to a rancher and had a young daughter, she couldn't always make sister lunches, but she was always reachable by phone.

Once they were all on, Stephanie brought her sisters up to speed and then got to the point of the call. "So, what should I do?"

"I don't see the problem," Tiffany said. "You're not dating anyone and he asked you out."

"And you said yes," Brittany added. "You can't back out now. That would be bad manners and plain wrong."

Stephanie rolled her eyes and even though she couldn't see her, she knew that Tiffany had rolled her eyes, as well. Brittany was the eldest and responsible to the nth degree.

"Stephanie, nobody is trying to hear about what Ms. Manners would say," Tiffany said, laughing. "And I've seen pictures of that man. If you're going to do wrong, he is definitely the person to do it with."

"Tiffany," Stephanie shrieked as her sisters laughed.

"The man does have a great body," Brittany added.

"Something as a married woman you shouldn't notice," Stephanie said.

"I'm not dead," Brittany added primly. "I can still look."

"I'm not married, so I can do more than look," Tiffany pointed out. "If you don't want him, give him my number. I'll take him off your hands."

"I didn't say I didn't want him," Stephanie said, fighting a surprising pang of jealousy. She knew her sister was just teasing. So why was she letting Tiffany get to her?

"Just as long as he doesn't turn out like that jerk Aaron you dated in college. He was all good looks on the outside and rotten to the core on the inside," Tiffany said.

"Of all the people I never think about," Stephanie said. "And Geoff is nothing like Aaron. That's not the problem."

"Then what is the problem?"

"The paparazzi," Stephanie said.

"In Bronco?" Tiffany snorted. "Girl, please."

"His accident was on the news. I don't want them following me and trying to take my picture and splashing it all over."

"Don't take this the wrong way," Tiffany said,

"but nobody cares that much about a small-town nurse. If they do follow you guys, it won't be because they want to take your picture."

"And if they do," Brittany added, "smile that gorgeous smile of yours and keep moving."

"What else is bothering you?" Tiffany asked. "We know there's more going on here or you wouldn't have alerted the cavalry just for a dinner date."

Stephanie hesitated. "What if I get too attached to him? He's not going to be in town long."

"You haven't even been on one date, so cross that bridge when you come to it," Brittany advised. "In the meantime, enjoy yourself."

Stephanie reminded herself of her sisters' words the next night as she got dressed for her date with Geoff. She reminded herself that he was from Bronco and that many people knew him and wouldn't be starstruck.

She put on her favorite gold knit dress that clung to her curves and a pair of gold ankle-high boots with three-inch heels. She took extra care with her hair and makeup, accentuating her eyes and her lips. When she was satisfied that she looked her absolute best, she put on a pair of gold hoop earrings, a matching bracelet, and spritzed on perfume. She was checking her appearance in a full-size mirror when the doorbell rang.

Right on time.

Stephanie hurried to open the door. She took one look at Geoff and her breath caught in her throat. His body had looked great in the casual clothes that she'd seen him wearing—heck, he'd even looked good in the hospital gown—but dressed in a navy suit and blue pinstriped shirt? Whew. He was off-the-charts gorgeous.

"Come on in. I just need to get my coat."

"Thanks."

He stepped inside and looked around. "Nice. Did you decorate it yourself?"

"Yes."

"I like the bold colors. They suit your personality."

"You think so?"

"Most definitely. Beiges and browns wouldn't work for you. They're too bland. Too neutral. You attract attention the minute you walk into a room."

"Says the man who has people following him everywhere he goes."

"That's a different type of attention. It has very little to do with me as a person and everything to do with my job. If I quit the rodeo and became a bank teller, eventually people would see that I'm a regular guy and lose interest in me. You, though, could never be ordinary if you tried."

Although she didn't agree with his assessment of either one of them, she nodded and grabbed her coat. "If you say so."

"Let me help you with that." He took her coat with his good arm and held it out for her. She could have put it on without his help, but she appreciated the gallant gesture.

"Thanks."

They stepped onto her porch, and she locked the door behind them. As she turned, she saw a black stretch limousine idling in front of her house. She raised an eyebrow as she looked at him.

He shrugged with his good shoulder. "I don't usually travel by limo or any other extravagant means. I actually own a nice sports car that admittedly doesn't get much use. But driving is out of the question with this arm."

"I see."

The chauffeur opened the back door for them and once they were safely ensconced inside, he drove away. Stephanie sat back against the buttery soft leather seats. She didn't quite feel like Cinderella riding in a carriage, but this came close.

"Where are we going for dinner?"

"The Coeur de l'Ouest. I heard that it's very nice, so I thought we'd go there."

Nice was an understatement. DJ's Deluxe, a high-end rib place, was nice. The Association, a private cattleman's club for local ranchers, was on an even higher level. But Coeur de l'Ouest? That was the fanciest restaurant in the state and well out of reach of her nurse's salary. It had only opened recently, but with its classically trained chef and reputation for elegant service, it had quickly earned a fabulous reputation. If Geoff was trying to impress her, he was off to a good start.

"That sounds great to me."

They chatted companionably on the drive to the restaurant. When they arrived, the chauffeur once more opened the door for them. Geoff held out his good arm for her, and they quickly walked the cobblestone path to the front door. A stiff Montana wind blew and she moved closer to Geoff to share his warmth since the cold didn't seem to bother him and the awning covering the walkway did little to protect them from the elements.

A uniformed doorman was standing beside the wooden door and he opened it for them as they approached. They thanked him and then stepped inside.

Geoff gave his name to the hostess, who immediately led them to their table. While they followed the woman through the dining room, Stephanie took the opportunity to look around. The decor was exquisite. Clearly no expense had been spared. Enormous crystal chandeliers dangled from the high ceiling. Their light, combined with the light from the candles on the tables, provided the perfect ambience.

Thick carpet muffled their footsteps as they crossed the room. When they reached their table, covered in pristine white linens, Geoff held her cushioned chair for her before he sat down across from her. The silver was heavy and obviously expensive, the glasses of the finest crystal. So far the restaurant had far exceeded her expectations. Of course, this was simply window-dressing. It wouldn't matter how luxurious the surroundings if the food wasn't tasty. But from the aromas filling the air and the blissful expressions on the faces of the other diners, that wasn't going to be a problem.

The restaurant had a fixed menu which was sitting beside the plate. Stephanie perused it, trying to ignore the fact that people were staring at them. She tried to muster a smile as Brittany had suggested, but she couldn't pull it off. She ordered herself to focus on the printed words and not the phone cameras aimed at her table. She wasn't going to let a bunch of strangers ruin her evening. That decided, she turned to Geoff. "So tell me. How are you enjoying your return to town? And what are your plans?"

Geoff heard Stephanie's question and took a swallow of water before looking back at her. He'd been anticipating tonight ever since he'd convinced her to have dinner with him. The day after he'd been freed from the hospital, he'd checked on the availability of reservations and had been assured that a table would be made available for him whenever he chose to come. Although he wasn't one to use his fame to get special treatment, when it came to this date with Stephanie, he wasn't going to look a gift horse in the mouth. He knew the value of a first impression and he wanted to make it a good one.

Although his ankle was well enough to comfortably walk, he'd nearly fallen over when her door had swung open and he'd seen her standing there. In that moment he'd realized what the term "breathtakingly beautiful" truly meant. She'd taken his very breath away. Of course he'd known she was attractive. But the shapeless pale blue scrubs she'd worn at the hospital hadn't done her justice. She was made for that gold dress.

And her face. He could barely tear his eyes away from it. She had the most beautiful skin he'd ever seen in his life and once more he'd been sure she was a celestial being. No mortal being could be so perfect. He could lose himself in her rich brown eyes. They were so expressive, reflecting her every emotion. He wondered just how many feelings he could arouse in her if given the time.

He shook his head. He wasn't going to go there. This was not going to be a long relationship. He didn't do those. And emotions weren't going to be involved. At best, this would be a fling. A holiday affair. When he was healed, he was going to have to work extra hard to regain his competitive form.

He might want to keep in touch with Stephanie, but he wasn't going to have a moment to spare. Not if he intended to stay ahead of the competition. All the more reason to enjoy their time together now since it was going to be short.

"No? No to what?" she asked, and he realized she must have thought his head shake was an answer to her questions.

"Sorry. I wasn't answering you."

"So, what…you were shaking your head to make sure all the rocks were still in there?"

He laughed. "Something like that. And before you ask, none of them are missing."

"That's good. I would hate to think they didn't survive the accident."

The accident was the last thing he wanted to talk about even if it was the reason he and Stephanie had met. "My visit is going okay," he finally said.

She nodded, but seemed dissatisfied by his answer.

"It's not going according to plan," he elaborated, "but there's nothing I can do about that. I'm doing my best to work around the injury. Fortunately the photographer managed to get enough shots of me before the bleacher incident, so the promotion for the Mistletoe Rodeo wasn't affected."

"I noticed that the media only had a couple of shots of you on the gurney as you were being wheeled to the ambulance, and those were taken from a distance. How did you manage to pull that off?"

"It wasn't me. The press was made up of people that have known me for years and they respected my privacy. As for the other people on-site that day? The manager of the convention center and a couple of local politicians were in the building when the accident occurred. I think they put the fear of God in everyone present. If even one picture was leaked to the press, there would be hell to pay. That threat didn't extend to people on the street, though. Still, I'm not bothered by it. I was more worried about my family finding out that I'd been hurt before I could reach them. I didn't want them imagining the worst. Once they knew that I was okay, I didn't care about the pictures."

"Doesn't it bother you to have your every move scrutinized? Don't you feel a little bit…I don't know…strange being watched all the time? Like a bug under a microscope?"

"Nobody has referred to me as a bug before."

She grinned. "Maybe not to your face."

He laughed. "True."

"But seriously, people are looking at us right now and a few have even snapped pictures with their phones. They're trying to be discreet, but I have to tell you it's a little bit unnerving and it's making my skin crawl."

He shrugged. "It goes with the territory. True,

most rodeo riders aren't big celebrities and live normal lives under the radar. And to be honest, I wasn't expecting this level of attention when I chose my career. That's not at all what I was looking for. But since I use that same fame to sell products and put money in my bank accounts, I can't very well complain. That would make me a hypocrite, something I don't want to be."

Though he had signed up for the ever-present media, and the surreptitious videos that people made of him with their phones, Stephanie had not. Moreover, his fame had grown over time, so he'd had the opportunity to get used to it. She was being thrust into the limelight suddenly.

But there was more to him than Geoff Burris, celebrity athlete. He was a three-dimensional man. Hopefully before this evening was over, he'd be able to show her the other side of his life. The regular Geoff, son of two beloved educators, who'd grown up in the same town as she had.

The waiter arrived right then, ready to serve their first course. Geoff's nerves jangled as the waiter set down their plates. He hoped that Stephanie would enjoy the dinner. He really wanted this night to be perfect.

"This looks absolutely divine," Stephanie said. She lifted the fork to her mouth and the morsel of food disappeared between her full, kissable lips. The moan of pleasure that she made hit him in the gut and his imagination began going places that it shouldn't go, at least not on a first date.

"How does it taste?" he asked, although he had a good idea of what she would say.

"Like heaven. Seriously good."

He tasted his own oysters and had to agree. "No wonder this restaurant has a waiting list. I was a bit surprised, given that it's off the beaten path."

"Yes, but do you see those views?" Stephanie pointed out the window beside them. The mountains were visible in the distance, but they almost seemed close enough to touch. Although the restaurant had lots of windows, they had clearly been given the best table in the place.

"The view is absolutely beautiful. At least it is from where I'm sitting," Geoff replied. Stephanie might have been talking about the mountains, but he was talking about her. She was a vision who grew more beautiful with each passing moment. He couldn't imagine how gorgeous she would be in, say, thirty years. *Whoa. Slow down there, cowboy.* They didn't have thirty days much less thirty years. There wasn't room for a long-term relationship in his life.

Stephanie turned and caught him staring at her. "Did you even look?"

"Yes. Like I said. Beautiful."

She smiled as she caught his meaning.

As they ate one delicious course after another,

they talked about everything under the sun. She wasn't a fan of sports and he didn't like the sci-fi shows she enjoyed, but they both watched a serialized program with a lot of intrigue. As they ate their chateaubriand, they debated over who would turn out to be the villain. He'd been sure of his position in the beginning, but after listening to Stephanie's arguments, he was almost ready to change his mind.

As they perused the three options on the dessert menu, he noticed Stephanie staring over his shoulder. Geoff turned around and a man immediately put down his cell phone, giving Geoff a rueful smile. He turned back to Stephanie, who blew out a breath.

"Come on. We're having a great time," he said. "Don't let anything change that."

"You're right. And for the most part, I forgot that we're eating dinner in a fishbowl. At least you are. Most of the attention is focused on you. I only get the occasional glance, as if people are trying to figure out if they've seen me before. When they realize I'm nobody famous, I'm sure they start to wonder who this regular girl is having dinner with you."

"You got all of that from a glance here and there?"

She laughed. "Okay. I might have embellished the storyline, reading a lot into a look, but it doesn't take much imagination to figure out that's what they're probably thinking."

"I doubt it. I think they were wondering how one guy could be lucky enough to have a great career and be eating dinner with the most gorgeous woman they've ever seen."

She shook her head. "I doubt that's the case. I'm just glad I don't have to live like this all the time. Don't get me wrong. I'm having a great time. Dinner was fabulous. This was the best food I've ever eaten." She flashed him a mischievous grin that made his pulse race. "And the company wasn't too shabby, either. But I don't think I could tolerate being the center of attention like this. I like my privacy too much."

He understood. But his life wasn't like this all of the time. Sure, fans who recognized him acted as if he were something special. To them, seeing him in person was a big deal. But his family and friends didn't treat him like that. To them, he was just a regular guy. She just hadn't seen that side of his life.

They finished their dessert, which was just as delicious as dinner had been, and he paid the bill. "How about a nightcap?" he asked as they walked to the limousine.

She smiled at him with perfectly straight white teeth and his heart jumped. He was used to jolts of adrenaline—when he was on the back of a bucking bronc. But from a simple smile? That shouldn't have affected him the same way. But it was Stephanie's smile.

"I'd love one," she replied. "What did you have in mind?"

"I thought we'd go to a little place I know. It's not exactly exclusive, but not many people in town go there."

"That sounds mysterious. And intriguing. I'm in."

Geoff instructed the driver on where to go and then leaned back against the leather seat. He pressed a button and soft music filled the secluded area of the car. Stephanie crossed her ankles and then smiled at him. "You know. I could get used to this."

So could he. He knew that she was talking about the chauffeured limousine, but he was thinking about having her in his life. And that was a problem.

Chapter Five

Stephanie glanced out the limo window and then over at Geoff. He was staring at her as if gauging her reaction. The building they were parked in front of was worlds apart from Coeur de l'Ouest. While the restaurant had been an elegant establishment, serving those with highbrow tastes who wouldn't bat an eye at its if-you-have-to-ask-you-can't-afford-it prices, this place was a hole in the wall. And that was being generous. The storefront didn't even have a sign out front. You definitely had to know it was here in order to find it. The outside might not look like much, but she'd been raised not to judge a book by its cover.

She wondered if Geoff was testing her. Was he trying to see whether she would refuse to go inside? Did he think she would turn her nose up and demand that the chauffeur drive off? If so, he was in for a big surprise. "Is this it?"

"Yep."

"What's it called?"

"Doug's. It doesn't look like much, but it's my favorite place to hang out when I'm in town."

"Okay. Let's go."

He smiled and she knew that if it had been a test, she'd passed. She briefly considered becoming offended, but decided against it. It had to be hard being rich and famous and being unsure if people liked you for who you were or for what you had.

Stephanie wasn't looking to get ahead or take advantage of anyone, but Geoff had no way of knowing that. They'd just met. Only time spent together would reveal the type of people they were. Not that they would be spending a lot of time together. Geoff had made it plain that he wasn't looking for anything long-term. That was fine with her. She was perfectly willing to have a brief fling. As long as they were honest with each other, neither of them would get hurt.

When they stepped inside, she looked around. Although the exterior left something to be desired, the interior was clean, and the furniture looked comfortable. Scarred wooden tables and chairs lined the walls in the front room with a jukebox standing in one corner. A pool table, currently in use, and a bar were at the far end of the room with what she supposed was a dance floor in between. A solitary chair with a piece of caution tape draped across it was shoved into a corner. What was that about?

"Hey, Geoff," a man called from across the room.

"Hey, Boone," Geoff called back. He took her by the elbow and led her across the room. "These are some of my friends. I've known Boone, Dale and Shep Dalton since they moved to town. They live on a ranch outside of town called Dalton's Grange."

"Nice to meet you," Stephanie said.

"You, too. Pull up a chair, Geoff," Boone said, rising to give his seat to Stephanie.

Geoff grabbed an unused chair from a nearby table and then sat down. A waitress came over and Geoff and Stephanie ordered soft drinks.

"I'll be right back with them," the waitress said.

"I know you've been out of town for a while," Boone said, a grin on his slightly wind-burned face, his blue eyes sparkling with mischief, "but the dress code hasn't changed in that time. Jeans and boots would have been fine."

"You're just as funny as I remember, which is not much," Geoff said with a grin. "We went out to dinner before coming here."

"Don't mind him," Shep said. "He's just trying to change the subject from Sofia Sanchez."

"Who?" Geoff asked. He glanced at Stephanie as if she were supposed to know who Sofia was. She shrugged. She had no idea who the other woman was.

"His girlfriend. We were just talking about when they were going to start having children."

"No, that's what *you* were talking about. I was just enduring in pained silence," Boone interjected. "And I know that Stephanie and Geoff don't want to listen to you guys drone on about my life any more than I do. Besides, my hands are full right now with Spot. She's all I can handle right about now."

"Who's Spot?" Stephanie asked.

"She's sort of my dog."

"How can she 'sort of' be your dog?"

"Last month this dog showed up on my ranch. I'd never seen her before and I don't have a clue where she belongs. She's not chipped so there's no way to find her family. So I sort of adopted her."

"You could have dropped her off at the Happy Hearts Animal Sanctuary. Daphne Taylor takes great care of her animals. She has everything from cows and pigs to cats and dogs, so Spot would be quite happy there."

"I could have, but doing that didn't set right with me. Spot came to me. She could have gone anywhere, but she sought me out. She needs me."

"And you take her everywhere. Like you would a kid," Shep said, shaking his head.

"You brought the dog in here?" Stephanie

asked. Suddenly she remembered hearing about a stray dog wandering around town. The dog had become something of a sensation and most of the town had been talking about it. Of course, the Daltons lived out on their ranch and she didn't know how often they came to town. Perhaps they hadn't heard the talk. "Can I see her?"

"Sure."

"I'll come, too," Geoff said. "I want to meet your dog."

Boone led them to a corner of the joint where a dog was lying on a blanket, gnawing on a squeaky chew toy. She lifted her head when they approached her, momentarily forgetting about the rubber bone. Stephanie smiled as she knelt before the dog. "Aren't you a cutie?"

She scratched behind the dog's ears and then glanced over at Geoff. He squatted and petted the dog who instantly began to lick him affectionately. Obviously the dog had good taste. Stephanie watched as dog and man lavished each other with affection. So Geoff was an animal lover.

Stephanie stood and looked at Boone. "I think this dog might be Maggie. You should call Daphne and have her come see."

He frowned. "Who is Maggie?"

"She's the dog who won the Bronco's Pet Contest on the Fourth of July. She ran away before anyone could get ahold of her. She's been seen all over town. People have tried to catch her, but she's too fast and no one has been able to hold her."

Boone looked at the dog, and Stephanie could tell that the animal had won his heart. He didn't have to worry about his ability to be a good father when the time came. Clearly he had a lot of love to give. "I'll think about it. No promises, though. Like you said, she ran away from other people. She *came* to me. And who knows, Spot might not be Maggie."

"That's true. Just think about calling Daphne, okay?"

Boone nodded. Geoff rubbed the dog one last time before getting to his feet. Taking Stephanie's hand in his, he led her back to the table. They passed the stool behind the caution tape and her earlier curiosity returned.

"Why is there a stool in a corner with caution tape on it? It doesn't look broken."

"Oh, that? That's just the haunted bar stool."

"The what now?"

"The haunted bar stool. Don't tell me you've never heard of anything being haunted before?"

"Of course I have. Houses. At Halloween. And my sister Brittany worked at Bronco Ghost Tours for a hot minute. But stools? That's a first for me. Is there a story behind it or did someone just decide to throw caution tape over it as a way to attract customers to the bar? Or maybe it's some kind of conversation starter?"

Geoff chuckled. "There's a story behind it. From what I hear, people think it's cursed because bad things happen to customers after they sit there."

"Like what?" As a nurse, she was a believer in science. All this other mystical, magical stuff? That was for the superstitious types.

"Well, I didn't see anything happen firsthand. I've just heard the stories," Geoff admitted.

"Rumors. I know how they get started. One little bit of truth can be magnified and twisted until it's unrecognizable. Like that game of telephone when we were kids."

"It's true," Doug Moore, the owner, piped up from behind the bar. He looked to be in his late eighties, but he moved with the ease of a much younger man. With alert eyes, he seemed sharp as a tack. Not the type to believe in haunted furniture.

"Really? Okay, I'm curious now." Geoff might not have firsthand knowledge, but Doug should. It was in his establishment after all.

Doug stopped wiping the bar and leaned against it, pushing a bowl of olives out of the way. "There was a guy who sat on that bar stool. He'd been happily married for nearly twenty years. That very night he went home only to find his wife had left him and filed for divorce."

Stephanie wondered just how much time that

man had spent perched on that stool tossing back bottles of beer instead of at home with his wife. Maybe that was the cause of the divorce. But she kept that comment to herself and simply nodded.

Doug must have taken that nod as agreement because he plucked an olive from the bowl and popped it into his mouth. He chewed slowly for a second before continuing. "And then there was that poor unfortunate guy who went bankrupt." He ran a hand over his close-cropped gray hair and looked around. "What was that fella's name?"

"Henry Jamison," several people called out. Either they'd heard this story before or they'd known the man. Stephanie would put money on the former.

"That's right. Henry Jamison," Doug repeated. "Now see, Henry had a head for business. Some people are born with that gift and Henry was one of them. He was a bit of an investor. Knew what to invest in because it was going to take off and what to sell because it was going to go bust. He even gave me a stock tip here and there. He was right every time. I've never seen anyone with that talent before or since. Anyway, he came in here one day and sat on that stool. Before the week was out he was flat broke. Lost every red cent he had to his name in a stock deal gone bad. He left town not much later and no one has seen or heard from him since."

What could she possibly say to that? A man lost money playing the stock market. It happened all the time. Surely as a businessman, Doug would know that.

As if sensing that she was still skeptical, Doug leaned across the bar, making sure he had her full attention. "Then there was that poor guy who died."

"From sitting on the bar stool?"

"Yep."

"Did he fall off and hit his head?"

Doug rolled his eyes at her suggestion as if it were too pedestrian to warrant any other response.

"I take it that's a no."

"Correct. Bobby Stone. He'd been healthy as a horse. Then he sat on that bar stool and three days later it was all over. He just dropped dead." Doug swiped a hand across his shiny forehead. "They said he had a heart attack while he was up on the mountains—he might have been rock climbing, but I never got the whole story, and they never found his body after he fell. But I knew the real truth. It was the bar stool."

Stephanie looked at Geoff and the Daltons and finally the other patrons. Was this some elaborate joke? Were they pulling her leg? Waiting for her to believe it so they could laugh at her for being gullible? She didn't get that feeling from any one of them. Quite the opposite. They looked like believers. Or at least not doubters.

She turned back to Geoff who winked and shrugged his one good shoulder.

"Maybe it was all a coincidence," Stephanie said finally. "That would seem more logical."

"There's more to life than what can be explained," Doug said seriously. "Like that old TV show, *The Twilight Zone*, said. There are more dimensions than we know."

Stephanie regularly watched reruns of the show and knew that wasn't quite the way the saying went. Not that it mattered. She didn't base her reality on fictional television shows. "Well then, why do you keep the stool? Instead of putting it behind caution tape, why don't you just get rid of it?"

"No can do," Doug said, then chuckled. "You might think it's a little bit foolish for an old man like myself to be superstitious, but I've lived long enough to know there are some things that can't be explained. I may only have a high school education, but I'm smart enough not to pooh-pooh things just because I can't understand them. I certainly can't put the bar stool outside in the trash where some poor, unsuspecting person might take it home and sit on it. No sirree bob. I have to keep it right here where I can keep an eye on it. I keep my patrons safe by warning them about the chair."

Stephanie nodded. Who was she to ridicule his sincerely held beliefs?

"I'm not superstitious," Geoff said, jumping to his feet. Stephanie turned to him in surprise. He had been the one who'd first mentioned the stool being haunted. "I'll go sit on it."

"You don't have to do that," Stephanie said, grabbing ahold of his good arm. She thought the whole thing was just an urban legend, but why chance it? He'd already gotten hurt at a photo shoot, of all things. If that wasn't bad luck, she didn't know what was. Why take an unnecessary risk? She wished she'd never asked about the stool and that they could get back to having a normal conversation with the Daltons and the other people she'd met tonight.

"I know I don't." Geoff stepped around her and walked boldly to the chair. Every eye in the room followed him and other conversations faded away until an eerie silence filled the room.

"I wouldn't try that, son," Doug said as he shook his head. "You might end up with another busted arm or worse."

Geoff didn't hesitate or even slow down.

"But then, you young people have to learn the hard way," Doug said with a heavy sigh.

Geoff reached the chair and dramatically ripped away the tape. Then he sat on the stool and…nothing happened.

"See? Nothing to it."

"Well, I didn't expect your arm to fall off right this minute," Doug said. He grabbed the rag and began wiping the wooden bar again. "But don't be surprised if something bad happens to you in the next week or so."

"I'll keep that in mind," Geoff quipped, getting up and replacing the tape on the chair.

"You didn't have to do that," Stephanie said when Geoff rejoined her. "I didn't believe it was hexed."

Geoff laughed. "I know you didn't. But it was time somebody sat in that chair."

"Why did it have to be you?"

"Because nobody tells Geoff Burris what to do," Boone said with a grin.

"That's as good a reason as any," Geoff replied. He crossed the room and then put a coin into the jukebox. He stared at it for a minute and then pushed a button, making a selection. A moment later, a popular song filled the air. As one, people jumped up from their chairs and headed to the tiny dance floor. Geoff came back to the table and held out his hand to Stephanie. "Let's dance."

"What about your arm? And your ankle?"

"The ankle is much better. It doesn't hurt at all. And I don't need two arms to dance."

"All right," she said, taking his hand and standing, "but you'd better not make me look bad."

"Challenge accepted."

They joined the crowd on the dance floor. Stephanie had to admit that Geoff had some moves. Despite the fact that one of his arms was in a sling, he held his own. One song bled into another as other people fed coins into the jukebox.

Stephanie shimmied her hips as she raised her arms over her head. Geoff reached out and grabbed her hands, attempting to twirl her. He winced and then groaned. It didn't take a medical professional to know that he'd forgotten about his injury and had hurt himself.

"Careful there, cowboy. Remember you just had surgery. You need to take it easy for a while."

"I've been taking it easy," he gritted out between clenched teeth. "I'm tired of taking it easy."

"I imagine you are," she said in her most soothing voice. "But that doesn't change anything. The fact remains that you need to be careful with that arm. Don't overexert yourself. Take it easy for a few weeks and then you'll be back to normal."

"I don't have a few weeks. I need to be ready to perform at the Mistletoe Rodeo. It's less than two weeks away."

"I don't want to be the one to burst your bubble, but that's not going to happen."

"Thanks for the vote of confidence," he said, dropping her hand and stepping away from her.

"It has nothing to do with a lack of confidence

in you and everything to do with medicine. Your injury was severe. You won't be magically cured in a couple of weeks."

"Sure."

This conversation was getting them nowhere. It was futile to attempt to change Geoff's mind. That wasn't her job. Let him believe what he wanted just like Doug believed in the curse of a haunted bar stool. Neither of their beliefs affected her life one way or another.

"Are you ready to go?" Geoff asked, his voice cool.

"Yes," she replied in a tone just as chilly as his had been.

They said their goodbyes to Geoff's friends and then walked stiffly to the waiting limousine, each careful not to brush against the other. Neither of them spoke on the ride to Stephanie's house. What had started as such a wonderful date had ended in disaster. Stephanie wondered if maybe there had been a bit of truth to the haunted bar stool after all. It certainly had killed the evening and possibly her relationship with Geoff.

Geoff insisted on walking Stephanie to her front door and making sure that she was safely inside before he got back into the limo and instructed the driver to take him back to his parents' house. Stephanie's sweet scent lingered in the car and as he inhaled the perfumed air, he couldn't stop himself from recalling the highlights of their date.

Stephanie was much better than he'd expected her to be. He'd known from seeing her in action that she was a competent medical professional who cared about her patients. She was warm and had a way of getting difficult patients—namely him—to follow the doctor's instructions. She was classy and he'd known she'd be right at home at a five-star restaurant. But he had been pleasantly surprised by how naturally she'd fit in with the crowd at Doug's place. Doug's wasn't exactly a dive, but the joint didn't cater to the same clientele as the Coeur de l'Ouest.

He liked the way she'd interacted with his friends. The Daltons had teased Stephanie and she'd given as good as she got. He hadn't expected her to be as witty and funny as she turned out to be. She'd made a great impression on his friends. When she'd stepped away from the table, Boone, Shep and Dale had asked him if he and Stephanie were exclusive or if they were dating other people. The question hadn't set right with Geoff, although he'd smiled. He wasn't looking for anything serious, but the idea of Stephanie dating someone else had soured his stomach. But being jealous was so ridiculous it was laughable. Only he hadn't laughed then. And he wasn't laughing now.

Stephanie wasn't his girlfriend. Nor was she

going to be. After the way the evening had ended, he wasn't even sure if they were still friends.

So why was she still on his mind when he had other things that needed his attention? Like getting in shape to perform at the Mistletoe Rodeo. The rodeo was important for the entire town of Bronco, not just him. It would bring in a large crowd and was going to be telecast live on television stations across the country, something that was rare for rodeo. This was the chance to show a broader audience that rodeo was a sport for everyone, not just ranchers.

His presence was a big reason that television executives were suddenly interested in rodeo. Geoff wasn't conceited about the role he played, but he understood his influence. Over the past couple of years, as his popularity had transcended the sport, Geoff had become the face of rodeo. He'd seen his name linked to greats in other sports. He'd been given the opportunity that so many before him, namely his heroes Bill Pickett and Nat Love, had been denied. He wasn't going to let their memories down.

When he was a kid, his grandfather had taken him to the Bill Pickett Invitational Rodeo. He'd been so impressed, he had never forgotten what he'd seen. Or the pride he'd felt. He'd learned a lot about the Black riders who'd come before him and wanted to do his part to bring recognition to their accomplishments. He couldn't very well do that while sitting in the stands. He had to perform. And he would. He just wished Stephanie understood how important it was to him.

The driver reached his parents' home. After settling the bill and giving the driver a tip, he went inside the house. Fortunately no one was around and he made it to the kitchen without having to talk. He filled a glass with tap water and then went to his room where he swallowed his pain medicine. He was loath to admit it, but his shoulder still bothered him, even more so tonight. Clearly he'd overdone it. He'd gotten caught up in the moment dancing with Stephanie and had forgotten that he'd been injured. Attempting to twirl her had been a mistake that he'd instantly regretted.

If the throbbing in his shoulder was anything to go by, he might need to take it easy for a couple of days. If that was the case, he owed Stephanie a huge apology. He just hoped it wasn't too late to repair the damage he'd done. And not just to his arm.

Chapter Six

"So, how did it go?"

Stephanie grimaced at Brittany's voice. She'd managed to keep a smile on her face all day at work despite the disappointment she still felt about the way her date with Geoff last night had ended. A few of her coworkers were still curious about the beautiful bouquet he'd sent, and they peppered her with questions. Lucky for her, there were numerous patients that needed care so there wasn't much time to talk or think about Geoff. Apparently, now that she was home from work, that reprieve was over.

"It was okay."

"Uh-oh. That doesn't sound good. What happened?"

The concern in her sister's voice was nearly Stephanie's undoing, and tears filled her eyes. This was ridiculous. It wasn't as if she and Geoff had been involved in a relationship. They'd only gone on one date. True, she'd had more fun with him than she'd had with most of the other guys she'd dated over the past couple of years, but that didn't change the fact that it had been one date. She blinked back the moisture, refusing to let even one tear fall.

"I'm not really sure. It started out great. Dinner at Coeur de l'Ouest was fantastic. Afterwards we went to this bar he knew for a drink. One minute we were dancing and laughing and the next he was upset because I told him he needed time to recover from his surgery. It was as if he blamed me for his injury."

If she lived to be a hundred, she would never understand how men could be so pigheaded. Especially when it came to their health.

It didn't matter how macho or determined you were, the human body needed time to heal. And the healing process wasn't going to speed up just because he'd made a commitment to participate in a rodeo. To believe otherwise was magical thinking. Like believing a bar stool had the power to ruin someone's life. It just didn't happen. Geoff had to know that.

"Did he say that or are you just interpreting his actions?"

Stephanie sighed. "He didn't say it in so many words. In fact, he didn't say much after that. His attitude killed the moment and we just left."

There was a long silence. "So what are you going to do?"

"I'm not going to do anything. We went on a

date and it didn't work out. Now I'll go back to my regularly scheduled life, which doesn't include Geoff Burris." Just saying the words made her heart ache, but she pushed the pain aside. "I've lived twenty-nine years without him. I'm sure I can continue to do so."

"It's not always possible to go back. Daniel and I had a rough spot in the beginning of our marriage and I moved back into my place for a couple of days. Even though we hadn't been married long, I missed him like crazy. If we hadn't worked it out, I would never have gotten over him."

"But this was only one date, not a marriage. You were already in love with Daniel. I'm not in love with Geoff. I'll be over him in no time." She hoped.

"I thought that you liked him."

"I did. Despite the fact that he's famous, he seemed like a real down-to-earth guy. He took selfies with the food-service guy in the hospital. And he was great to everyone we met yesterday. We were having so much fun. I thought this could be the start of something. But then he turned around and acted like a jerk to me."

"Maybe he hasn't accepted the fact that his healing might take more time than he wants to believe and he took his fear out on you. He's probably sorry."

Stephanie snorted. "If he was sorry he could have called me and apologized."

"Men can be slow. He might need a little time to figure it out."

"What's to figure out? It's two words. *I'm sorry.* No, Geoff Burris is now a part of my past. I won't be thinking about him any longer."

"I hope it works that easily for you."

"It will."

After they ended the phone call, Stephanie leaned back against the sofa. If only she felt as confident as she'd sounded. But she had a sneaking feeling it wasn't going to be that easy to get over Geoff. Maybe she shouldn't have said anything last night. She would have been better off letting him hurt himself and then saying *I told you so.*

But *he* wouldn't be. As a nurse, she could never stand by silently watching while someone hurt himself. Heck, she couldn't do that even if she wasn't a nurse. She'd been raised better than that, raised to care about her fellow man. And it was even harder to watch someone you cared about hurt himself and be powerless to stop it.

Oh, no. Had she actually just thought that she cared about him? When did that happen? How was that even possible? They barely knew each other.

It took time for relationships to develop, for feelings to grow and trust to be nurtured. Perhaps she was confusing physical attraction with affection.

There was no denying that she was attracted to Geoff. What woman wouldn't be? His body was muscular with not a hint of fat. His face was gorgeous. But she was attracted to more than his outward appearance. She liked the type of man he was inside. His character. Or at least the man she thought he was.

While she was sitting there brooding, the phone rang. No doubt Brittany had called Tiffany and now her younger sister was calling to cheer her up. She grabbed the phone from the table without looking at the caller ID. Ordinarily she'd be happy to talk to her sister, but she wasn't in the mood to rehash things. "Hello."

There was a pause. "You sound…uh…busy. Did I catch you at a bad time?"

Geoff. After the way the date ended, she hadn't expected to hear from him again. Her heart began to pound and the blood raced through her veins. Perhaps last night hadn't been the end of the road for them.

"No. I just finished talking to my sister, Brittany. To be honest, I thought you might be my other sister calling."

"If this isn't a good time, I can call you back later."

"No, right now is fine." She paced to the mirror and then checked her hair. When she realized what she was doing, she rolled her eyes. It wasn't as if he could see her. And if he could, so what? This was how she looked after a day at work. She was a nurse, not a fashion model.

"Good." He cleared his throat and there was a long pause. "I'm calling to apologize for my behavior last night. I was rude to you and you didn't deserve that. I took out my frustration on you. After the way you helped me through my tough times at the hospital, you are the last person I should have been rude to. That was no way to repay you for your kindness. I'm sorry."

Her heart dropped to her feet. Was that what the flowers and last night's date had been about? Repaying her for doing her job? Why was she surprised? Had she really believed he was interested in her? He was one of the most famous athletes in the world and she was a nurse in a midsized Montana town. They lived in two different worlds. Somehow the fairytale-believing little girl she'd once been had convinced the woman who knew better that they were on the way to starting a relationship.

And he'd been repaying a perceived debt.

She somehow managed to keep the disappointment from her voice. "I understand. And I forgive you. Don't give it a second thought."

"I don't think it will be that easy to get out of my mind." He paused again, but she waited for him to continue. "The thing is, I know you were telling me the truth. I don't often meet someone who is willing to do that. So often people in my world tell me what I want to hear. I really appreciate your honesty."

There it was again. Thanks. She didn't want his gratitude. She wasn't sure what she wanted from him, but it wasn't that.

"No worries," she managed to say.

"I want to ask a favor."

"What's that?"

"I want you to promise me that you'll always level with me and that you'll never tell me what you think I want to hear."

Stephanie's heart lifted and then soared. Geoff wanted her to remain in his life. For how long, she didn't know. But even a short period of time would give them the opportunity to get to know each other better and decide whether they wanted to pursue a relationship. But as she recalled what he'd said about not having a place in his life for romance, she reminded herself not to fall in love with him.

"That's going to be an easy promise to keep. I'm a big believer in honesty."

"So am I," Geoff said, "just in case you were wondering."

She hadn't been, but she appreciated him saying so.

They talked about their days for a few minutes. As they chatted, Stephanie relaxed. He was so easy to talk to.

"What are you doing this weekend?" he asked.

"I don't have any plans. Why?"

"I was hoping we could spend some time together. I have to stop by the convention center Saturday and see what's going on. After that, I'm free."

"That sounds good. I need to do some housework, but that shouldn't take long."

They talked a few minutes longer before saying goodnight. Long after they'd ended the call, Stephanie's mind was filled with happy thoughts. She and Geoff were going to hang out together that weekend. She could hardly wait.

Stephanie checked her reflection in the mirror as she waited for Geoff to arrive. They'd talked again and firmed up their plans for the day. They were going to walk around town and check out the Christmas decorations and maybe do a little shopping for their families and friends and then go to DJ's Deluxe, Stephanie's favorite restaurant. Her sister Brittany had held her wedding reception there. The restaurant wasn't typically used for receptions, but Brittany was a creative event planner. She'd worked her magic, turning the dining room into a fairy-tale wonderland.

Not that Stephanie was thinking about a wedding reception. She was just looking forward to having a good dinner. And though she'd enjoyed Coeur de l'Ouest the other night, she would prefer not to be stared at while she chewed her food. DJ's Deluxe was popular with the locals who hopefully wouldn't be starstruck by Geoff and spend the evening watching them.

After assuring herself that there wasn't a speck on her orange asymmetrical hem, lace-up sweater or fitted jeans, she pulled on orange knee-high boots. A few strands of her hair caught in her large hoop earrings and she was untangling them as her doorbell rang. Stopping for a last glance at herself in the hall mirror, she picked up her lipstick and hesitated.

As teenagers, her brothers Ethan and Lucas had often complained that lipstick looked good, but it ruined kissing. They hated ending up smeared with it. She didn't know whether they felt the same as adults or if other men felt the same. Not that it mattered, she told herself as she put down the lipstick. Making out with Geoff today wasn't on the agenda.

She pulled the door open to find Geoff leaning against the doorway. He was dressed casually in a blue plaid shirt and dark blue jeans. And of course boots. His black leather jacket was only zipped halfway.

She'd convinced him that he didn't need to hire

a chauffeur. She had a car and didn't mind driving. Now he turned and waved at the driver of a truck idling in front of her house. The driver honked the horn and pulled off.

"Who's that?" she asked as he stepped inside.

"My brother Mike. He dropped me off."

"That was nice of him."

"It's what brothers do."

"How much grief did he give you?" she asked. When he shot her a surprised look, she shrugged. "I have brothers and I know how they treat each other."

"I forgot you told me that. He only gave me a little bit. But then he's been giving me a hard time all week so perhaps he decided to have mercy on me." He grinned. "Or maybe it was me reminding him of all the times I drove him around so he wouldn't have to go on dates with his mother behind the wheel."

She grabbed her coat and keys. When they got into her car, she turned to look at him. "Where to first?"

"I've been gone so long I'm practically a tourist. Take me to some of your favorite places. That is, assuming you have favorite places."

She laughed. "Of course I do. But I'm not sure they're quite what you have in mind."

"What do you mean?"

"My favorite places to visit are the boutiques.

I love clothes, shoes and boots. Then there's the spa. There's nothing quite like spending my day off getting pampered. A facial, massage and pedicure make for a perfect day."

"Yeah. That's not what I had in mind."

She grinned at him. "I got you covered. Let's go to Bronco Java and Juice and get some hot chocolate. Then we can walk around and you can get reacquainted with the town again. To be honest, this is a great time to pretend to be a tourist. With all of the Christmas decorations going up, the town feels so festive."

"That sounds like a plan." He held out his arm and she took it.

As they walked to her car, visions of the day ahead of them danced in her head and her heart skipped a beat. She could definitely get used to spending time with Geoff.

"Do you want to drink in here or walk around?" Geoff asked once they held their drinks.

"Let's walk," Stephanie said. "At least until I start to get cold."

Geoff smiled at her. "Don't worry. I'll keep you warm. I have heat to spare."

Stephanie laughed. "I'll keep that in mind."

"Which way do you want to go?" he asked as they stepped outside.

She pointed to the right and they started down

the street. The wind blew, and Stephanie stepped closer to him. Her sweet scent wafted around him, filling him with sudden desire.

"I love the way Bronco looks during the holidays." Stephanie sounded so delighted he had to smile. "Once they finish with everything it's going to be a winter wonderland."

Although Christmas was a few weeks away, several municipal employees were busy adding holiday decorations to the streetlights. Six-foot lighted snowflakes were being hung from the light poles on one side of the street while toy soldiers were being hung from light poles on the other side. Several business owners had also gotten into the act, stringing colorful lights around the windows of their establishments. To be honest, Geoff didn't ordinarily pay much attention to things like this, but when he looked at the town through Stephanie's eyes, he felt some Christmas spirit.

When they finished their drinks, they tossed their cups into the trash. He took her hand in his good one as they strolled around the street.

"How are things at work?" he asked. Reporters constantly asked about his life. Fans did the same. As a result, he constantly talked about himself. He would much rather talk about Stephanie. And he was genuinely curious about her life. Her job was more important and valuable to society than his would ever be. She spent her time helping to save lives and caring for the sick. He spent his days and nights trying to stay on the back of a bucking horse.

The light from her eyes faded. "Yesterday could have gone better. One of my patients took a turn for the worse and had to be moved to ICU. I'd thought that she was on her way home. Now, though..." She shrugged, and he felt the sorrow rolling off her in waves. Obviously she wasn't in it just for the paycheck. She genuinely cared for her patients.

"So, what now?"

"Now we wait and see. Hopefully her health will improve just as quickly."

"I'm sorry for bringing it up and making you sad."

"Don't be. I appreciate that you asked. Most people don't."

Though he was sorry people didn't often ask about her day and her patients, he was happy that he'd separated himself from the pack. He wasn't interested in anything serious, but he didn't want to be lumped in with the other men she'd known. He didn't want to be one of many. He wanted to be one of *one*. That thought shook him to his core and he wondered where it had come from. He wasn't looking for anything long-term. When he left town, it was over. So why did it matter whether he stood out?

"I do care. Just like you promised to tell me the truth, I promise you that I'll always be willing to listen to you."

Her smile was so broad and bright it nearly blinded him. She squeezed his hand and leaned closer to him. Her sweet perfume wrapped around him, reaching him in places that had been off-limits for the longest time. "Thank you."

They were nearly at the corner when Geoff heard a man calling Stephanie's name. She turned and her eyes lit up, and he was attacked by the green monster. He really needed to get hold of this uncharacteristic jealousy. Preferably before the two men walking in their direction reached them.

"What are you guys doing here?" Stephanie asked, hugging one and then the other.

"Just checking out what's in the stores," one of them answered.

The men looked from Stephanie to him.

"I'm sorry. Let me introduce you. Geoff, these are my brothers," Stephanie said. She pointed at a man with a trim beard and shoulder-length locks. "This is Lucas." Then she pointed at the man with close-cut hair and glasses. "And this is Ethan."

Her brothers. Relief flooded his veins, and he smiled.

She looked at Geoff. "And this is Geoff Burris."

Geoff smiled. "It's good to meet you."

"Same here," Lucas said.

"Sorry about the arm," Ethan added. "Hopefully it will be better in time for the rodeo."

"Are you rodeo fans?" Geoff asked.

"Oh, yeah."

"Let me set you up with tickets," Geoff said.

"That would be great," Ethan said.

"I'll get them to Stephanie."

"Sounds good."

"We'd love to talk more," Lucas said, "but we're meeting some friends at Bronco's Brick Oven Pizza."

"It was nice meeting you both," Geoff said, waving as they went their separate ways.

"Thanks for the tickets," Stephanie said. "My brothers are going to have a great time."

"I have a ticket for you, too. I hope you'll come." He knew she wasn't a fan, but he hoped he could convert her.

"I would love to."

They walked around for a few more minutes. Although she was dressed warmly, Geoff knew she had to be getting cold. The day had started out sunny, but the sun had been gradually replaced by clouds as they'd walked.

Stephanie smiled. "I'm having a great time, but I'm getting a bit chilled, and I don't have hot chocolate to keep me warm."

He could keep her warm. All he needed was the chance. Despite his intention to keep their relationship strictly platonic, images of them spending time alone in his bed flashed in his mind, and he smiled. Realizing that Stephanie might be able to figure out what he was thinking—it wouldn't be hard to do—he then wrapped his good arm around her waist. "Then let's get to DJ's so you can get warm."

As they went, snow flurries began to fall. Some landed on Stephanie's shoulders.

She shivered and glanced at him from head to toe. "I'm dressed in boots, coat and hat, and you're only wearing a jacket. I can't believe you're not cold."

He could. Being around her aroused him and he felt as if a four-alarm fire was raging inside him. The cold Montana air didn't stand a chance of cooling him off when Stephanie Brandt was around. Especially wearing those sexy, if impractical, orange boots. She provided the color in an otherwise ordinary day.

The drive to the restaurant was short and before long they were standing inside DJ's Deluxe. They were waiting to be shown to their table when he heard his name being called. Turning, he saw his brothers Mike and Ross walking toward him. What were they doing here?

After rushing home to be with him after the accident, canceling events of their own, they'd decided to stay until after the Mistletoe Rodeo. He appreciated their concern, but he didn't want to spend time with them tonight. He wanted to be alone with Stephanie. Besides, it was Saturday night. His brothers were popular with the ladies. Shouldn't they be on dates?

"Hey," he said. "What are you guys doing here?"

"We both had a taste for ribs and decided to come here." Ross looked from him to Stephanie and Geoff had no choice but to introduce them.

"Stephanie, these are two of my brothers, Mike and Ross." He gestured to his brothers. "This is Stephanie Brandt."

"It's nice to meet you," Ross said, and Mike seconded that.

"You, too," Stephanie said.

"We were hoping to get a table, but it looks like we're going to be waiting a while," Mike said.

"You can join us if you want," Stephanie said graciously as Mike had probably known she would.

Geoff shot his brother a dirty look, willing him to decline the offer. Mike grinned and exchanged looks with Ross, and Geoff could practically read their minds.

"If you're sure you don't mind," Mike said. Ross's shoulders shook as he struggled to hold back his laughter, and Geoff began plotting ways to get even with his brothers.

Stephanie turned her gaze to Geoff who smiled. What else could he do? "We don't mind, do we,

Geoff? I know how long the wait can be on a Saturday night if you don't have reservations."

"Then we accept," Mike said.

The hostess approached them at that moment. "Table for two?"

"Four," Ross said.

The hostess looked at Geoff for confirmation, and he nodded. He'd made a reservation for two but knew because of his blasted fame that they'd accommodate the two additional people. Besides, the tables were large enough to fit four easily.

As they followed the hostess to the table, Geoff stepped close to Mike and muttered, "When you least expect it, expect it."

Mike only laughed. He was the most easygoing of all of the brothers. Geoff knew that when he got his revenge, Mike would take it good-naturedly.

Geoff held Stephanie's chair and then sat beside her. Although his brothers were all too pleased with themselves for horning in on his date, they were incredibly nice to Stephanie. Not that he expected anything less of them. They were good guys. Whenever they met up on the tour, they often double-, triple-, or even quadruple-dated. Those times had been fun and filled with laughter.

But unlike those occasions when he hadn't minded sharing his date with other people, he wanted Stephanie all to himself. He didn't want her dividing her attention between him and his brothers.

"So, how do you like being a nurse?" Mike asked after they'd perused the menu and placed their orders.

"I love it." Stephanie's eyes glowed, and Geoff's breath stalled in his throat. Every time he thought he'd gotten used to her stunning good looks, he looked at her and was once again struck by her beauty. He forced himself to look away from her so he could breathe again. His eyes met Ross's, and his brother gave him a knowing look. Geoff frowned. He didn't know what his brother thought he saw and he didn't want to know.

"I'm going to medical school," Mike said.

"Really?" Stephanie said. "Joining the doctors, huh? Is there anything I can do to convince you to join the nurses on the cool side?"

"No, sorry," Mike replied with a grin. "I'm working on the rodeo circuit to save money for tuition. Medical school is ridiculously expensive."

"I know," Stephanie agreed, and she and Mike talked about medicine and what it was like to work in a hospital. "If you have time, stop by and I'll introduce you to some doctors I work with. They'll be better able to tell you what to expect than I am."

"I will. Thanks." Mike smiled.

Stephanie might be unaware that she'd just won

over two of his brothers, but Geoff knew it and was unexpectedly pleased.

Stephanie excused herself to go to the ladies' room, and Ross smiled. "Now I understand why you insisted on having her as your nurse."

"How did you find out about that?"

"Mom. She thought it was sweet."

Geoff could pretty easily guess what else his mother was thinking. And plotting. No doubt she was hearing wedding bells and imagining becoming a grandmother in the near future.

"I just thought—"

"She was a good nurse," his brothers said in unison.

"We heard that before," Mike said. "And after talking with her I believe it's true."

"Thank you," Geoff said, hoping to put an end to the conversation.

"But she is gorgeous," Ross added, clearly unwilling to end the conversation until he'd said his piece. "And really nice."

"I never denied either of those things." Geoff saw Stephanie crossing the room, returning to the table. "And since she's on her way back, let's drop the subject."

"Geoff has a girlfriend," Mike said in a singsong voice and Ross laughed.

There were no two ways about it. His brothers were annoying children.

Stephanie reached the table and they all stood as they'd been raised to do. Once she sat down, they did the same. She looked around. "What did I miss?"

"Nothing," Geoff said, answering before either of his brothers could.

"Fine. Don't tell me. But remember, I have brothers so I can recognize those smiles from a mile away. You three were definitely up to something."

Mike opened his mouth as if to speak and Geoff kicked him under the table. Mike jumped and laughed uproariously. Thankfully, the waiter arrived with their food right then and the conversation halted. Once they began to eat, they talked about other subjects. Time flew as they laughed and told stories.

When the bill came, Ross insisted that he and Mike split it. "After all, we crashed your party. It's the least we can do."

"Thanks," Geoff said. "I appreciate it."

Once the bill was settled and Geoff left a nice tip for the waiter, they put on their coats and went to the door.

"So, do you want to come home with us?" Mike asked. "That way we can save Stephanie the trip."

"I don't mind dropping you off," Stephanie said.

Geoff felt like his fifteen-year-old self on his first date. Only this was worse. So much worse.

"How about we stick to our original plan," Geoff said to his brother. "I'll call you from Stephanie's when I'm ready for you to pick me up."

"That works, too," Mike agreed.

They said their goodbyes and as they went to their respective cars, Geoff said, "I hope you don't mind that I invited myself over to your place."

Stephanie smiled. "I was hoping you would come back for a while. I just didn't want to inconvenience your brother."

"They owe me. I chauffeured them many times when they were teenagers so they wouldn't have to be driven around by our parents."

"You're a good brother. It's clear that they love and admire you."

"I don't know about all that," he replied. As the oldest, it had always been up to him to set the right example and he'd done his best to do right by them.

"I do."

They reached her car and as they drove to her house, all thoughts of his brothers vanished to be replaced with one thought. He was going to have more time alone with Stephanie. He intended to make the most of it.

Chapter Seven

Stephanie's heart began to race as she led Geoff into her living room. They were completely alone and she was a bit nervous. The drive here hadn't taken long and she'd been acutely aware of him every second of it. His cologne had floated over to her, enticing her with every breath she took. He smelled so good. Even though it had grown colder by the hour, the heat from his body had reached her, slipping around her like a warm blanket.

She flipped a wall switch, and the lamps on either side of the sofa turned on, providing ample light, while simultaneously casting a romantic glow.

Geoff struggled to remove his jacket, and she controlled the urge to help him. It didn't take a genius to realize that he hated being dependent on anyone. When his brother had offered to drive him home, he'd bristled as his pride had taken a hit. He'd done his best to cover it, but she was beginning to recognize his expressions and moods. She'd seen him at his lowest—in pain and vulnerable—and his true nature had been revealed. He was a good—and proud—man.

"Would you like a nightcap?" she asked and then grinned as she recalled how he'd said similar words to her the night they'd ended up at Doug's.

"What do you have?" he asked as he draped his jacket over the back of a chair.

"Wine. Beer. Hot cider or cocoa."

"I'll take a beer."

"Coming right up. I'm going to have something warm."

"That doesn't surprise me. You definitely don't like the cold."

"It shows, huh?"

"Oh, yeah."

She headed to the kitchen and was surprised when he followed her. The kitchen was a good size, but his presence was so enormous that the room suddenly felt small. Intimate. She grabbed a bottle of beer from the fridge and twisted the cap before handing it to him.

"Thanks."

She pulled a carton of milk out as well and then closed the refrigerator door with her hip. After grabbing sugar and a can of cocoa from the pantry, she put a pan on the stove and set to work.

"None of that instant stuff mixed with water for you." Geoff leaned against the counter, watching.

His lips lifted into a half smile that sent tingles down her spine.

"No way. I'm not a fan of chocolate water. Some people unwind with a glass of wine, and I do occasionally when it's warmer, but hot cocoa is my go-to drink when it's cold. Given that I live in Montana where it's freezing a great deal of the time, my drink has to be the real thing."

"Have you ever considered moving somewhere warmer?"

She shook her head and stirred her cocoa, heating it slowly. When it reached her preferred temperature, she poured it into her favorite mug and added a handful of mini marshmallows. She turned off the stove and led him back to the living room where they sat on her sofa. Once they were comfortable, she elaborated. "I was born here. My family is here. I can't imagine living anywhere else."

"But there's so much world to see." He set his bottle on a coaster on her coffee table and then angled his body toward her. The motion brought them closer together, and his thigh brushed against hers, ramping up the desire that she'd been feeling for him all evening. "The world is so big. There are so many experiences to be had. I don't think there's enough time to do and see everything."

"I didn't say I never left Montana. I have. I've taken wonderful vacations and plan on going on even more. But at the end of the day, I'm a small-town Montana girl."

"There's nothing wrong with that. Small-town Montana girls are my favorite."

She arched an eyebrow. "Is that right?"

He nodded. "There's something about them that just appeals to me. They're so irresistible. Or at least one of them is."

Her heart, which had picked up its beat when his thigh touched hers, began pounding out of control, and the blood raced through her veins.

Geoff took her mug and then set it on the table next to his beer. He reached out and caressed her cheek, and she sighed. Although his hand was calloused, his touch was exceptionally tender. He moved slowly, cautiously as he closed the distance between them. Their gazes held and she read the question in his eyes. She nodded, barely percep- tibly, and he kissed her.

His lips were gentle as they brushed against hers, giving her the opportunity to back away. Moving away was the very last thing on her mind. She didn't want distance. She wanted to get closer to him. Closing her eyes, she wrapped her arms around his neck and deepened the kiss. Yearn- ing roared through her, but a part of her knew she needed to take it slow.

As if reading her mind, Geoff pulled back slowly and she opened her eyes and met his gaze. His deep brown eyes appeared almost black. "I've wanted to do that from the moment I laid eyes on you. Of course back then, I wasn't sure you were actually real."

Stephanie leaned closer and kissed him briefly. "I've been hoping that you would do that. But I guess we should stop before things get out of control."

"Not what I want to do, but it's wisest given the circumstances."

This was a temporary fling and neither of them wanted to end up with permanent heartache. Stephanie nodded. Stopping might be the smart thing, but it definitely wasn't what she wanted to do, either.

Geoff entered around the convention center, eager to take a look around. For the past few days, he'd been working tirelessly to publicize the rodeo. He'd done phone interviews, radio interviews and Zoom sessions with reporters from all over the country. Anything he could do to draw attention to the Mistletoe Rodeo. And he was willing to continue to do so until the actual date if it meant more people would attend in person or watch on television.

The center was beginning to take on the familiar appearance of many rodeo arenas he'd competed in across the country. The chutes and pens were being erected along two walls. The dirt hadn't been put on the floor yet and Geoff had been told it would arrive sometime tomorrow. The organizers had assured Geoff and the other competitors that it would be quality dirt with the appropriate depth and mixture. Although it wasn't a big deal to the audience, dirt was extremely important to the competitors.

Geoff's blood began to race through his veins as his excitement grew. This was where he belonged and where he felt most comfortable. There was nothing quite like rodeo. Nothing came close to the rush he felt on the back of a horse, competing against some of the best bronc riders in the world to get the highest score. More times than not, he'd done just that.

He moved his injured arm, testing how much range of motion it had. Not as much as he liked but there was a marked improvement. He'd had a follow-up examination with the surgeon this morning, and the doctor had been surprised and impressed by the rate at which Geoff was improving. Still, he warned Geoff against moving too quickly. In his estimation, Geoff wasn't well enough to perform in the rodeo.

Geoff disagreed. The rodeo opened in four days and he was going to be a part of it. It was going to be a three-day event. Since he was acting as master of ceremonies and doing television commentary, Geoff was only riding once, and that was on the third day, which would give him seven more days. That was time enough to heal.

"So, this is where the rodeo will be held?" Stephanie asked as she approached him. "It looks just like your standard convention center."

Geoff smiled as he looked at her. He'd invited her to come with him to see the changes in the arena. She had to work this afternoon, so they'd agreed to meet before she went in. He kissed her cheek before answering.

"Haven't you ever been to a rodeo?"

She shook her head. "Never."

How was that possible? She lived in Montana, for goodness' sake. "Never?"

"Not once. It never appealed to me. Now though, listening to you talk about it and seeing how excited everyone is, I'm beginning to believe that was a mistake."

"Wait until it actually starts and the building is rocking with the energy of thousands of fans. You'll find yourself cheering along with them."

"I don't know about all of that, but I'm willing to give it a chance. Especially since the master of ceremonies is so cute."

He found himself blushing, something he'd never done in all his life.

"Wait until you see me ride."

She frowned but didn't say anything. He knew she didn't approve of his performing so soon after surgery and he appreciated the fact that she respected him enough not to try to dissuade him. His parents had been married for almost thirty-five years. Growing up, Geoff had had plenty of time to watch them navigate difficulties. One thing he'd learned from observing them was how important mutual respect was to any successful relationship. *Whoa.* There he went again, thinking about having a permanent relationship with Stephanie. Even more startling was the fact that the thoughts included marriage. He didn't want to start thinking about Stephanie in those terms. What they shared was only temporary. That's all it could be right now. Anything else would be too complicated.

That was why he'd pulled back the other day when he'd kissed her. Kissing Stephanie had felt so good. So right. And for a brief moment he would have given anything for the right to kiss her for the rest of his life. That thought had shocked him into slowing down. It was too soon for him to be having those kinds of thoughts. Besides, there was no place for a woman in his life, no matter how right Stephanie had felt in his arms.

He'd kissed many women in his life but had never felt with any of them what he'd experienced with Stephanie—emotionally or physically. Even now, just being so close to her and inhaling her sweet scent aroused him and awakened emotions that he wasn't ready for. He needed to focus on the rodeo and not the sexy woman currently beside him, her arm wrapped around his good biceps. But when she was near, thinking of making a future with her didn't seem as outrageous as he knew it was.

"Let me show you the rest," Geoff said, eager to distract his racing thoughts.

They'd just completed the tour when the door opened and a group of reporters came in for a scheduled press conference. He glanced over at Stephanie, trying to gauge her reaction. He wanted her to stick around while he talked to the reporters, but he didn't want to ask her to stay if she didn't feel comfortable doing so. If he asked, she might say yes out of obligation even if she preferred to stay anonymous.

He was used to having his picture taken and it didn't bother him. It was part and parcel of being the face of rodeo. But he didn't want to violate Stephanie's privacy. She should be able to live her life out of the spotlight if that was her preference. But if they were going to be together, she might not always have a choice. It was only a matter of time before someone photographed them together. It was better to ask her now how she felt so he could make accommodations in the future if necessary.

"How do you feel about having your picture taken? I'm not saying anyone will. I'm asking just in case. Will that bother you?"

She met his eyes. "No. I guess I don't mind."

He smiled. "Okay then."

Geoff led Stephanie to the area that had been cordoned off for the press. She chose to stand a few feet away from the reporters. It wasn't very formal, with him standing behind a podium, addressing them as if he were the president. He loathed those kinds of setups. Today they just stood in a circle talking about the Mistletoe Rodeo.

"How's the arm?" someone asked. "Will you be able to ride?"

"It's on the mend. And I will most definitely be riding." Geoff saw Stephanie frown at his response, but he didn't qualify his answer. They'd just have to agree to disagree.

As a nurse, she believed the doctor should have the last word. But Geoff knew his body better than any doctor ever would. He was confident he would be fine.

After the press conference, Stephanie had to leave so she could get to work on time. As much as he wanted to spend more time with her, Geoff walked her to her car and kissed her goodbye. "I'll talk to you later."

"Later," she repeated and then drove away.

He waited until she'd driven from the lot and then returned to the convention center. He'd only been inside a few minutes when he heard his name being called. Turning, he saw his friend Brandon Taylor walking in his direction. Geoff had recently signed a sponsorship deal with Taylor Beef, Brandon's family business. As part of the arrangement, Geoff was going to shoot TV commercials, record promotional radio spots and do print ads and billboards. Of course, the injury to his arm had necessitated pushing the schedule back a few weeks. He didn't want to be in a sling when he shot the commercials. Luckily he'd planned on being in town for a while, so changing the date hadn't created a lot of complications.

"Hey, Brandon," he called to his friend. They'd attended high school together although Brandon had been a year ahead of Geoff. Back then, Geoff had been envious of Brandon's popularity with the girls. Every girl in school seemed to have set their hearts on Brandon. Geoff hadn't been as lucky. Most girls had barely noticed him. And those that had, slotted him in the friend zone. Once he became a rodeo star, his luck had improved.

"Geoff. Got a minute?"

"Yep. I'm here all day. I'm in between press conferences and rehearsals."

"This is turning into a bigger event than I thought possible," Brandon said as they shook hands. "I have to say I'm impressed. I know you're big in rodeo, but I saw national press outside. Bronco is definitely going to be on the map after this. Thanks to you."

"I can't take the credit. Bronco has been Montana's biggest secret for far too long. And rodeo has been growing in popularity for a while. It's just perfect timing. But you didn't come here to talk about rodeo, did you?"

"Nah. I haven't seen you for a while and since I was in the area, I thought we could catch up. How's the arm?"

"Better, but to be honest, it's the last thing I want to talk about."

"Understood."

"But it will be better in time to shoot the ads."

"I have no doubt about that."

They talked about old times for a while, reminiscing about the exploits of their younger days. "What's going on with you, Brandon? Are you still breaking hearts all over town?"

Brandon laughed and then smiled sheepishly. He ran his hand through his dark hair and his slightly ruddy skin grew red. "Actually, I'm engaged."

"What? Are you serious? Congratulations! Who's the lucky lady? Is it someone I know?"

"Do you remember Cassidy Ware? We dated briefly in high school. She was two years behind you. She owns Bronco Java and Juice now."

Geoff thought for a minute and then shook his head. "The name sounds familiar but I can't picture her face. But then, I wasn't as popular with the ladies as you were."

"We're going to have a baby."

"Wow. Talk about jumping in with both feet. Who would have thought you'd be settling down?"

Brandon laughed. "Certainly not me. I wasn't looking for anything serious. It just kind of sneaked up on me. One minute I was living my life and the next I was madly in love. You just never know."

Unbidden, a vision of Stephanie popped into Geoff's mind. Could he be ready for something serious with her? He wasn't sure. Sometimes he couldn't picture life without her. But they were still getting to know each other. Their lives were so different. It would take a lot of effort and compromise to make it work. Although he hated to admit it, she might not want to get serious with him.

"Well, you seem happy," he told his friend.

Brandon smiled broadly. "Happier than I've ever been."

"Bring her around. I'd love to get to know the woman who has changed your life."

Brandon nodded. "I will."

"Hey," a voice called.

"Hey, Dean," Geoff called back to Dean Abernathy. Being in town was giving him the opportunity to catch up with people he hadn't seen in a while. "What's going on?"

"You mean since you decided to go with Taylor Beef instead of Abernathy Meats?"

Geoff laughed and held up his hand in front of him. "It was a hard decision."

"But in the end, he made the right one," Brandon joked.

"Well, it was a *decision*," Dean said. "I'm not sure it was any better than choosing to sign with BH Couture. Who knew you wanted to be a fashion icon?

"By the way," Dean said, his blue eyes sincere. "Congratulations on your engagement, Brandon. There must be something in the water. My brother Tyler recently got engaged himself."

"Thanks," Brandon said, a goofy grin on his face again. No secret who he was thinking about. "When will it be your turn?"

"Never if I'm lucky. I've seen the way you guys have been reeled in. I'm doing my best to avoid getting that hook in my mouth."

"I hear you," Geoff agreed, although a part of him thought that being caught by Stephanie didn't sound all that bad. After all, she'd be caught, too.

"You're both pitiful," Brandon said. "You're two of a kind."

"Now we're pitiful?" Dean asked. "Before you and Cassidy got together, you thought the same way."

"Maybe. But I've seen the light and I'm going to walk in it."

"On that note, I'd better get to work," Geoff said. "I'll see you guys later."

As the three of them went their separate ways,

Geoff couldn't stop thinking about how happy Brandon looked at the idea of settling down and spending his life with one woman. Maybe Geoff needed to give the idea more thought before he dismissed it out of hand.

The next few days were full of activity and Geoff only had the opportunity to spend a few moments with Stephanie. Either he was at the convention center or promoting the rodeo or she was at work. But the rodeo started tonight. Although Dr. Wilson hadn't given his approval to perform, he had given him the go-ahead to drive.

He hopped into his car and then went to pick up Stephanie. She was waiting for him when he arrived, and she only needed to grab her coat before they were on the road again. As usual, she was dressed in a manner that accentuated her gorgeous curves—a form-fitting yellow sweater that ended at her waist and faded blue jeans that cupped her sexy bottom. She was wearing yellow high-heeled fashion boots that were extremely sexy if not practical.

Although he'd left in plenty of time to arrive at the convention center, traffic slowed down as he neared the building. Cars were lined up to get into the lot even though the first events weren't scheduled to start for a few hours. He was pleased that people were excited about bringing the rodeo to

Bronco. Once he reached the gates to the parking lot, he showed his identification and was directed to the reserved section.

They parked, went inside and looked around. Whoever had been in charge of the decorations had definitely overdosed on the Christmas spirit. No matter which way you turned, you saw a reminder of the season. There was holly everywhere and twenty-foot-tall Christmas trees in every corner. Groups of carolers dressed in silver-and-gold tops and black bottoms strolled around, singing familiar Christmas songs. There were countless concession stands selling mugs of hot chocolate or warm apple cider. The aroma of freshly baked cookies floated in the air and his stomach growled. Teenagers, dressed in red or green elf costumes, handed out candy canes to one and all.

"This is spectacular," Stephanie said, her eyes alight with excitement. "I had no idea it would be like this."

"Neither did I. It's definitely living up to the holiday theme, that's for sure."

They wandered around for a few minutes before they came upon mistletoe. Geoff pointed at it. "Well, lookie here. Mistletoe. You know what that means."

Stephanie giggled. "Geoff, the place is crawling with photographers. And people with phones."

"Nobody is looking at us," he said, not knowing if that was true, but doubting it. Someone was always looking at him. "Besides, it's tradition."

"Well…"

Geoff put his hand on Stephanie's waist and pulled her closer to him. Their eyes met and held and sexual tension arced between them. "One little kiss won't hurt anything."

She nodded and drifted closer. Geoff leaned over and brushed his lips across hers. Although he'd intended to keep the kiss light, the minute he felt her mouth beneath his, that vow flew out the window and he kissed her deeply. The feel of her soft breasts pressed up against his chest was nearly his undoing. She moaned softly and her sweet scent wafted around him, enticing him to hold her more closely. He felt bereft when she moved away, and he reluctantly ended the kiss.

He pressed his forehead upon hers while he tried to steady his breathing. Despite the feelings surging through his body and the slight guilt in his mind, he was pleased to note that Stephanie was just as breathless as he was. He lifted his head and stared into her slightly glazed eyes. Obviously she'd been affected by the kiss, too.

"Wow," she murmured.

"Yeah." He wanted to say something more, something to let her know how he felt, but for the life of him, he couldn't seem to think of anything else.

"Over here," someone called, breaking the spell. Geoff looked around and realized that they'd drawn quite a crowd of onlookers. Even some members of a television crew had gathered. It wasn't clear whether they'd filmed the kiss, but he imagined that everyone with a phone—and wasn't that just about everyone in the world these days—had probably taken at least one picture if not more.

Geoff glanced down at Stephanie, who pressed her face into his chest. Clearly she didn't appreciate having what was supposed to be a private moment between two people be witnessed by hundreds of strangers and which no doubt would soon be splashed over the internet. "Sorry about that," he whispered. "I didn't realize we'd become the center of attention."

"You definitely are a magnet."

The crowd began to surge around them and Katy, the convention center manager's assistant, came up to him and pointed at her watch. He looked back at Stephanie. He didn't want to leave her in the middle of their conversation, but this was part of his job. It was time to start the autograph session.

As if sensing his dilemma, she stepped back. "Go ahead. I'll just go find my seat."

"I'll try to stop by before the show if I get a chance."

She nodded and began to slip away. The urge

to hold her close suddenly struck him, but he suppressed it. He was being ridiculous. They were only saying goodbye for now. Not forever.

Stephanie had barely turned before she felt herself being pushed farther and farther away from Geoff. She looked back at him, but he seemed enthralled by what a pretty young woman was saying to him. The other woman had a possessive hand on Geoff's forearm and was smiling into his face. That didn't bother her. What did bother her was the way Geoff returned the other woman's smile. He was looking at her the same way he'd just looked at Stephanie. As if she and Stephanie were interchangeable.

"You aren't special. Did you think you were?"

It took Stephanie a moment to realize that the comment had been directed to her. She turned and looked into a pair of cold, gray eyes. "What did you say?"

"I said you might think you mean something to Geoff, but you don't. And he's not your property." The other woman swept her hand around the crowded concourse. "Look around. You're one of many. So if you want more of his time, take a number. But in the meantime, get out of my way."

Stephanie told herself that the other woman didn't know what she was talking about. After all, Stephanie had come here with Geoff. But as she looked at him, she noticed he was giving his sweet smile to yet another woman and her confidence waned. How many other women had he smiled at that way over the years? And how many more would be the recipient before the night was over? Stephanie didn't know and she wasn't about to stand around and count. After all, hadn't he said rodeo and relationships didn't mix? Clearly she was the only one even considering the possibility.

Pushing her way through the throng of eager women, she finally reached Geoff. He looked at her and smiled. Despite knowing she was no more special to him than any of the other women awaiting his attention, her heart skipped a beat. She stood on tiptoes and spoke directly into his ear so that he could hear her over the voices of the women. "I got a call from the hospital. I need to go in and cover a shift."

"Can't they find anyone else?"

She shook her head, telling herself that wasn't disappointment she saw in his eyes. Why would he be disappointed when he had hordes of adoring fans battling for his attention? "No. They tried everyone else."

"How will you get there?"

"I'll call for a ride."

"Okay. I'll talk to you later."

She nodded, but he'd already turned back to yet another woman. Obviously that hadn't been disappointment she'd seen on his face. It had only been a figment of her overactive imagination.

Just like the sudden shift at the hospital. It didn't exist. She'd made it up. Anything to get out of here. Even sitting alone on her couch would be better than watching Geoff pose for selfies with these underdressed and over-made-up buckle bunnies. Telling herself she wasn't jealous, Stephanie pressed through the throng and toward the exit. The farther away she got from Geoff, the fewer people there were and the faster she was able to walk. By the time she reached the doors, she was sprinting.

She called for a car and shivered in the lot until it arrived. Fortunately the driver wasn't any more interested in talking than she was, and the ride passed in quiet.

When she got home, she washed her face and changed into a pair of comfy fleece pajamas and grabbed a pint of Cherry Garcia from the freezer. Opening the ice cream, she wrapped a throw around her shoulders and turned on the television. There was a commercial advertising the rodeo and Geoff's voice filled the room. His baritone made her heart ache.

"Nope," she said, changing the channel until she found an old favorite romantic comedy. Only amateurs would be competing tonight and it wouldn't be televised, but she didn't even want to see Geoff's commercial.

Digging into the carton, she watched as two mismatched people argued and bantered before they finally fell in love. Too bad it didn't work that way in the real world where mismatched people eventually went their separate ways.

When that movie ended, she placed the empty carton and spoon on the table, snuggled under the throw and watched the next equally improbable sappy movie. This was so much better than standing around while Geoff smiled and flirted with countless other women. So much better. So why did her heart ache so much she could practically feel it breaking? She closed her eyes against the tears that threatened and tried to think of something else.

Somewhere in her haze she heard a ringing bell. Sitting up, she blinked and realized that the sound was her doorbell. She looked at the television. A man dressed in a white apron was extolling the virtue of a frying pan. He wiped it clean with a cloth and a hidden audience applauded. Her movie had ended and now infomercials were on. Clearly she had fallen asleep. What time was it?

Her doorbell pealed again and she stood, swiping a hand across her mouth. "Coming."

The television provided the only light as she crossed the room. She switched on the porch light and looked through the peephole. *Geoff.* She opened the door and then stepped aside, letting him in.

"Are you okay?" he asked. His eyes swept over

her body from head to toe. Despite herself, she shivered.

"Of course. Why wouldn't I be?" The darkened room was a bit too intimate for her liking, so she switched on the lamps and then turned off the television.

"When the rodeo ended, I went to the hospital. One of the nurses told me that you weren't there and that you hadn't been there all night."

"Oh." She hadn't expected him to check up on her.

"Yeah. Oh." His voice was flat. "I thought you might have been in an accident or something. And yet here you are perfectly fine." He stared at her. "Why did you lie to me?"

"I wanted to leave."

"Why? I know you said you don't like rodeo, but I thought you would at least give it a try. You left before you could see anything."

"I saw enough," she said, ignoring the disappointment she heard in his voice as she recalled watching him with the other women. Now she understood what he'd meant when he said rodeo and relationships didn't mix. It wasn't because of the nature of rodeo. Rather it was because there were too many women for him to settle with just one. And why would he when there were women willing to accept whatever pieces of himself he was willing to give? Tonight she'd been slapped in the face with that reality and she didn't want any part of it. "What's that supposed to mean?"

She clamped her lips shut so the truth wouldn't come spilling out. The last thing she wanted was to reveal how much he was coming to mean to her. How much it hurt to see him with those other women.

"So that's it. You're not even going to tell me what happened that made you leave?"

"You were so busy with your fans you barely noticed me." And she didn't believe he'd missed her when she was gone.

"You lied to me because I wasn't giving you enough attention? Is that right?" He sounded angry, as if he were the one who'd been cast aside in favor of strangers' adulation.

"Why does it matter? I'm surprised you even noticed I was gone. After all, there were plenty of other women there to take my place."

Chapter Eight

Geoff stared at Stephanie. Dressed in shapeless pajamas that she'd obviously bought for warmth, she looked sexier than she should have. Noticing how gorgeous she was right now made him even angrier. How could she stand there and accuse him of ignoring her when he'd made a point to include her in every aspect of his life from the day they'd met? He'd introduced her to his friends. She'd met two of his brothers. He'd taken her on a tour of the convention center. Furious words bubbled to the surface, but he managed to keep them from exploding from his mouth. Their relationship was already on shaky ground. Saying the wrong thing could shove it over the edge of the proverbial cliff.

He inhaled and tried to regain his cool. Counting to ten usually helped. He made it to three. "You do realize that interacting with fans is part of my job. In fact, if you would have bothered to read the program, you would have seen that an autograph session was part of the schedule, followed by a meet and greet. People like to interact with the competitors. It adds to the whole rodeo experience."

"And you were definitely giving those women a whole lot of personal attention."

"Are you kidding me?" He tried to keep from yelling, but he didn't like being accused of things he didn't do. Geoff knew lots of athletes took advantage of every opportunity a buckle bunny threw their way. He never had. Friendly and professional had always been his motto and he'd always been careful not to cross the line.

"Do I sound like I'm kidding?"

"You sound like you've lost your mind." He unfastened his jacket and yanked it off without feeling the slightest pain. If they were going to have a long argument—and from the way she folded her arms across her chest and plopped onto the couch they were about to do just that—he wanted to be comfortable. She kept the temperature in her house just this side of hell and he needed to cool down.

"Are you trying to tell me I didn't see what I saw? Or hear what I heard?" she said in a raised voice.

"I don't know what you think you saw or heard, but I know what I did. My job."

"So it's your job to let women paw all over you?"

Talking—or rather yelling—wasn't getting them anywhere. He went and sat beside her on the couch and took her hand. She snatched it away.

When she didn't get up and walk away, he counted it a win. Stephanie mattered to him and he didn't like seeing her angry—especially when he believed her anger was masking pain.

Their relationship was new and fragile. One misunderstanding could shatter it. Over time she would come to know that she could trust him. She would know that none of the women he'd taken pictures with mattered to him. But she didn't know that yet.

"No, Stephanie. But part of my job is to keep fans happy. My job requires me to do publicity. That doesn't just mean doing interviews and shooting commercials. It means spending time interacting with fans. Taking pictures and signing autographs. The Mistletoe Rodeo is important to me. It's also important to the town. So yes, I posed for pictures and smiled at other women. It's part of what I do. What I have to do."

She huffed out a breath. Since he appeared to be getting through to her, he continued.

"Right now the press loves me. Every story they write about me is positive. But that can change on a dime if I make a wrong move. The media scrutinize everything I do. And let's face it, there's always someone looking to make a name by bringing down an idol. I had to work so hard to get to the top. Twice as hard as others. And it's going to take just as much work to stay there. But if I made you feel like I didn't care for you, or that you were disposable, I apologize. You mean a lot to me, Stephanie. Let's not let a misunderstanding ruin what we have."

She sat still, appearing to weigh his words. Everything he'd said was true. He only hoped she'd heard the sincerity in his voice. Recognized the feeling behind his words. Because there was nothing else to say. Either he'd convinced her or the hadn't.

After a minute, the stiffness left her back and the anger seemed to seep out of her. She turned to face him. "I accept your apology. And I'm sorry for getting so upset. I should have told you how I felt instead of just leaving like that. I don't know why I lied to you."

"Maybe you were trying to protect your feelings?"

She nodded and looked down at her hands. "Yes."

He reached out and turned her face to his again. "I care about you, too, Stephanie. I know we haven't known each other very long, but it doesn't feel that way. When we're together I feel like I've known you forever."

"I feel the same way, too," she admitted. Her voice was soft. Sweet.

Unable to stop himself, and knowing darn well that stopping was the farthest thing from his mind, he leaned over and kissed her. The loneliness and disappointment he'd felt when she'd left the rodeo, the worry and fear he'd felt when he'd discovered she wasn't at the hospital, and the anger at her deceit all melded together, turning into intense desire. The kiss was hot—hotter than the kisses they'd shared before. As his tongue swept hers, he felt an all-consuming fire shoot through his body. The kiss deepened and hot flames licked at his brain and incinerated every logical thought. In no time he was burning with desire.

With great effort, he ended the kiss and held her close. "I want you so badly, Stephanie."

She nodded against his chest. "I want you, too."

"Are you sure? You're driving me crazy, but I don't want you to have regrets in the morning."

She kissed him again and he nearly lost control. "I won't have regrets. I know exactly what I'm doing and what I'm saying. I want to make love with you."

That was all he needed to hear. They joined hands and she led him to her bedroom. He cursed his injured arm, but he knew it wouldn't impede him from thoroughly making love to her. By the end of the night, Stephanie was going to know just how important she was to him and all of her doubts would be swept away.

"Wow," Stephanie breathed out some time later. Before she'd met Geoff, she'd believed she possessed an extensive vocabulary. But making love with him left her able to think only one word. *Wow.* But then, no other word adequately encompassed everything she was thinking and feeling. She'd never felt such passion in another man's arms. But Geoff made her feel more than passion. He awakened emotions in her that she had deliberately left dormant, fearful of setting them free. He made her believe in true love again. After a few bad breakups and several unmemorable relationships, that was nothing short of miraculous.

Geoff laughed. "You read my mind. That's exactly what I was thinking."

She lifted her damp hair off her neck and then looked at him. "I'm not hurting your arm, am I?"

"Believe me, I'm feeling no pain."

"Still, you need to be careful."

He nodded and his eyes drifted shut. "I promise. I won't move a muscle."

He was true to his word and after a few moments, he was asleep. As she lay in his arms floating off to dreamland, she thought of what had passed between them and her doubts vanished. She could trust his feelings for her. Feeling satisfied, she joined him in a blissful slumber.

"Wake up, sleepyhead."

Stephanie opened her eyes. Geoff was lying beside her, leaning on his good arm. She reached up and touched his face. "Good morning."

"Yes, it is. I need to get going. I have to be at the convention center early today. And don't you have to go to work?"

She nodded. Earlier in the week she'd traded shifts with another nurse so that she could attend the rodeo, but she needed to work this morning. "Yes. But I'll be at the rodeo tonight."

"And you won't run out on me again?"

"I'll stay. Cross my heart."

"That's good enough for me." He sat up, and she was pleased to note that he had more use of his surgically repaired arm. Resting and following the doctor's orders was doing wonders for him. He paused and turned back to her, his eyes shining as they met hers. "I have a question. What do you dream about? I mean, is there something you want that you wouldn't buy yourself? A special gift I can give you?"

She shook her head. Where had the idea of gifts come from? She didn't want anything from him. Taking a calming breath, she reminded herself that she didn't know what type of relationships he'd had in the past. Had the other women he'd dated expected him to buy them presents? Maybe he'd come to believe that was part of dating. "I don't want anything from you." She stopped and shook her head. "No, that's not true. I want your time and attention. I want to be with you."

He grinned as he got out of bed and pulled on

his clothes. "That's easy enough. Just try and get rid of me."

Stephanie put on her robe then walked with Geoff to the front door. He kissed her briefly then left. Stephanie watched out the window as he drove away. She had to shower and get ready for work, but a part of her was still living the wonder of last night. His touch had been so gentle. His kisses hot yet sweet. Making love with him had been everything she'd dreamed of—and some things she hadn't dared to dream. She'd never jumped into relationships quickly. Generally she liked to take it slow, getting to know a man. To her, that gave the relationship a better chance of succeeding. But with Geoff, everything had happened so fast. But then, since none of her past relationships had worked out, there might be something to be said for moving quickly.

As she dressed for work, she tried to keep her doubts at bay. She wasn't going to overthink things. She was just going to see where the relationship led.

"So how are things with the rodeo star?" Tamara asked as they sat down together for lunch. Stephanie's mind instantly went back to the last night and she smiled.

"That good?" Tamara asked with a knowing smile before she bit into her sandwich.

Stephanie didn't bother to be coy. Besides her

sisters, Tamara was her closest friend. "Better than I could have imagined. I feel like I'm dreaming, but don't want to risk pinching myself for fear I'll wake up."

"It's real. And after all the Boring Bobs and Selfish Stans you've dated, you deserve to be with a man who makes you happy."

"And he definitely does that."

"Long may it last," Tamara said.

Stephanie lifted her turkey sandwich in a toast. "Amen to that."

The rest of Stephanie's day flew by. Before she knew it, she was driving home. She took another quick shower and then dressed carefully. She'd noticed a lot of the women wearing Western-inspired clothing at the rodeo last night. Fringed blouses, fancy belt buckles and tight jeans appeared to be the standard uniform. Every woman had sported cowboy boots. Or was the right word *cowgirl* boots? They'd ranged from simple brown to peacock blue with feathers.

Stephanie's wardrobe didn't include anything that evenly remotely looked like what the other women wore. And to be honest, Western clothes didn't appeal to her. She had her own flair. Today she was wearing a fitted red-and-white sweater, black jeans and thigh-high red boots with her customary three-inch heels. She switched from her

functional work purse to a red satchel. Her one
concession to the cowboy style was a red cowboy hat she'd been given by one of her sorority
sisters years ago that had been gathering dust in
her closet.

Grabbing her coat and gloves, she called Geoff
to let him know she was on the way and then drove
to the convention center. After showing the VIP
pass he'd given her, she parked in the area reserved
for competitors and their guests and then went inside. To her surprise, Geoff was waiting for her
by the doors. The look in his eyes brought back
memories of last night and she blushed. He kissed
her deeply, and goose bumps rose on her arms.

"I didn't expect you to wait for me," she said
when she'd regained her breath. "I know you have
things to do."

"Nothing is more important than being here
for you."

Her heart soared at the sincerity in his voice.
"Thanks."

"But I don't have a lot of time."

She took her ticket from her purse. "I can find
my seat."

"No. That's not necessary. I have enough time
to do that."

He led her through the building and up to a
guarded door. Geoff held out the badge attached to
the lanyard around his neck and the security guard

smiled and waved his hand. "I know who you are. Thanks for the autographed picture by the way. My son slept with it under his pillow last night."

"You're welcome," Geoff said.

The guard unlocked and opened the door for them. Stephanie walked beside Geoff through a well-lit corridor. They reached another door and the process repeated itself, including the thanks for an autograph. This time the door opened to a flight of stairs. At the top was yet another door. This time Geoff opened it and led her into a VIP suite.

The spacious room had been decked out for Christmas, too. Holly and ivy covered every surface. Green wreaths were hanging from the walls and a festively decorated tree lit up a corner. A table in the center of the room held warming dishes filled with delicious-smelling food. There was everything from hot dogs and burgers to meatballs and rib tips. There was even a pot of chili. A smaller table contained hot and cold beverages as well as a selection of desserts. So this was how the other half lived.

A middle-aged couple Stephanie assumed were Geoff's parents were sitting in comfy-looking chairs in front of floor-to-ceiling windows overlooking the arena.

"Come meet my parents," Geoff said, confirming Stephanie's thoughts.

She was suddenly struck by a case of nerves,

but Geoff didn't seem to notice. He took her hand and led her across the room. The couple rose and smiled. "Mom, Dad, this is Stephanie. Stephanie, these are my parents, Jeanne and Benjamin Burris."

"It's nice to meet you," Jeanne said, and Benjamin echoed the sentiment.

"You, too," Stephanie said, feeling instantly at ease. Geoff's parents were friendly and welcoming.

"So you're the nurse that took care of Geoff," Jeanne said.

"I was one of many."

"But she was definitely my favorite," Geoff said, smiling.

"Knowing our son and the way he hates hospitals, I'm sure he didn't make it easy. You have our eternal gratitude," Benjamin added. "And of course, any apology that may be necessary," he added with a smile.

"Hey," Geoff added. "I was a perfect gentleman."

"He was," Stephanie added.

Geoff looked at his watch. "And on that note, I need to leave. Sorry to just run out on you. I'll see you after the show."

"Break a leg," his father said with a wink.

"Let's not," his mother said, giving his father a playful elbow in the side. "He's broken enough of everything for a while."

Stephanie smiled, mentally agreeing with Jeanne.

"I'm not riding tonight, which you know," Geoff said, kissing his mother's cheek. "Dad was just wishing me good luck."

"Well, he could have just said that," Jeanne said, grinning.

Geoff's parents were a hoot and obviously very good friends. They reminded Stephanie of her own parents.

Laughing, Geoff shook his head and looked at Stephanie. "Walk me out?"

"Sure." Stephanie took his outstretched hand. It felt so natural to walk by his side.

When they reached the door, he leaned his forehead against hers. "I hate to leave you alone like this."

"I'm not alone. Your parents are here. I get the feeling they're going to keep me entertained. Go do your announcing gig."

He kissed her, his lips lingering before he pulled away. With one last look, he left and jogged down the stairs. Stephanie waited until she could no longer see him and then returned to where his parents waited, smiles on their faces.

Geoff hurried down the stairs and to the backstage area. The moment he stepped inside, Darren, the television production manager, rushed over to him.

"When I couldn't find you, I started to wonder if you'd gotten cold feet and run out," the other man said, worried blue eyes standing out in his pale face. His thinning blond hair went in every direction, as if he'd been raking his hands through it.

"No way. I'm looking forward to this. I just lost track of time." It might have felt like time was standing still when he kissed Stephanie, but in reality it had kept moving.

"No worries. You did well in the rehearsal. I just want to review one more time before the show starts in case you have questions."

Geoff nodded as Darren went over everything they'd discussed over the past days. Although Geoff had been a part of rodeo for half of his life, this was his first time being on the other side of the event. He would start on the floor, welcoming the crowd inside the arena as he had yesterday. But unlike last night, which hadn't been televised, he would be welcoming the television audience, as well. During a pause in the action, which was also a TV commercial break, he would go to the booth above the crowd where he would do color commentary with a famous sports announcer. He'd met Steve at rehearsal a day ago and found him to be fun and professional.

A bell rang and excitement made Geoff's pulse race. It was time for him to get the show started.

His blood pumped hard through his veins and his heart sped up as he walked across the floor to the center of the ring. After he was in place, a spotlight shone on him and the buzzing in the crowd instantly turned into a loud roar that threatened to raise the roof. Several people in the audience called his name.

"I love you, Geoff," a woman called out loudly, once the cheers died down.

He grinned. "Thanks for that. I love you, too."

The crowd cheered again and he waited until they quieted down before continuing. "Welcome to day two of the inaugural Mistletoe Rodeo. If you thought yesterday was fun, let me tell you something. You ain't seen nothing yet."

The crowd roared again, and once again Geoff paused. The producer had anticipated this reaction and had built time into the schedule. "Today you'll see some of the best competitors in rodeo. Prepare to be excited and amazed by their skill and daring. Feel free to stand and cheer as loudly as you can for your favorites. And now, let's get the show started."

The spotlight went out and he waited for his eyes to adjust to the darkness before following the illuminated tape on the floor from the center of the arena to the television booth. He had just enough time to sit down, put in his earpiece and grab his microphone before the first rider came out of the chute. Geoff had never given more than a passing thought to the behind-the-scenes production of the rodeo, but now he appreciated how much hard work went into giving the audience the best experience possible as well as making sure the competitors were safe and presented in the best light. All while staying on schedule.

Geoff was tentative at first, not wanting to be critical or unfair to the competitors when he knew from experience how hard they worked. Riders put in hours of practice for a few seconds in the ring. One mistake and all of that work went down the drain. But he had a job to do and an audience to educate as well as entertain. People wanted to hear his opinion. After a while he relaxed, and he and Steve simply talked honestly. By the time the fifth competitor was ready to start, they had gotten into a comfortable groove. It was almost like talking with one of his brothers.

Before Geoff knew it, intermission had arrived. His brothers would be competing in the second half, so he wandered down to the locker room.

"We've been watching you on TV," Mike said. "You're doing great."

"Not too critical?"

"Nope. You're honest."

Geoff's other brothers nodded their agreement.

"That's good."

"Of course my opinion might change depending on what you say about me," Ross said.

"I'll have only the highest praise," Geoff prom-

ised. "As long as you don't ruin the family's reputation as winners."

"That's not even a possibility," Ross said.

Geoff wished them luck and returned to the
booth. The lights had been turned on in the stadium and his eyes went to the VIP suite where he'd
left Stephanie with his parents.

When he spotted her, his heart lurched. Although she wasn't close enough for him to make
out her expressions, he could see her arms gestur-
ing as she spoke to his parents. He wondered what
they were talking about. No doubt she was charming them in the same way she'd charmed his brothers. The same way she'd charmed *him*.

But he couldn't stand here daydreaming about
Stephanie. He needed to get back to work.

The second half was just as exhilarating as the
first. The only time he was nervous was when his
brothers were competing. Although he'd always
told his parents not to worry about him getting injured, the big brother in him never breathed easily until his brothers had completed their events.
Tonight was no different. He was proud that when
the night ended, they were atop the leaderboard
and had made the cut for tomorrow—even Mike
who was just in it for the tuition money.

"That went great," Steve said after they'd removed their microphones and earpieces. "You're

a natural. When you get tired of competing, you definitely have a future doing color commentary."

"Thanks for making it so easy for me," Geoff said, shaking the other man's hand. "See you tomorrow."

Although the competitive part of the rodeo was over for the night, Geoff's day was not near ending yet. There were still more autographs to sign and pictures to take. He thought of how things had gone last night with Stephanie and hoped that tonight would be better since he'd explained the necessity of spending time with fans.

As he walked to the area where fans were gathering, he spotted Stephanie and his parents near the edge of the crowd. A security guard was beside them. Telling his escort he would be back in a second, he skirted the fans and went over to them. He and Stephanie said goodbye to his parents. Once the two of them were alone, he turned to Stephanie.

"Is everything okay?"

"Everything's fine." She smiled. "I know you have to hang out here. I'm going to go home and let you do your thing."

That sounded ominous. "Stephanie, I—"

"It's okay. I know this is part of your job." She kissed his cheek. "Feel free to come by when you're done. I'll be waiting up."

He nodded. Now that sounded promising.

Chapter Nine

"I can't believe today is the last day of the rodeo," Stephanie said to her sister Tiffany. They were enjoying their twice-monthly spa visit. They'd already had facials and massages. Now they were sitting in the lounge area, waiting for Tiffany's nail polish to dry. Stephanie never got a manicure. She washed her hands dozens of times a day at work, and the polish wouldn't last more than a couple of days before it started chipping and looking tacky.

Tiffany looked over at Stephanie and shook her head. "I can't believe you're really that into the rodeo. I understand Lucas and Ethan caring. They like sports. And even Brittany since she's married to a horse rancher. But you? I don't see why you care so much. You hate sports."

"Are you serious?"

Tiffany laughed and elbowed Stephanie in the side, careful not to smear her pale pink nail polish. "No. I'm teasing you. With your new boyfriend being a star bronc rider, I knew you would be obsessed with it. It's just hard for me to believe that you're dating an athlete."

"He's not my boyfriend," Stephanie corrected. She didn't want to fool herself into believing she and Geoff were more serious than they actually were. That was a sure way to end up heartbroken. Unless and until he told her otherwise, she was going with the understanding that their relationship status hadn't changed even if her feelings had. They were simply having fun while he was here. When he went back on tour, they'd return to their regularly scheduled lives.

"Whatever you say."

Tiffany's phone buzzed. It was on the table between them, but the polish on her nails wasn't quite dry. "Can you get that for me? I don't want to smudge my nails."

"You don't mind me seeing your messages?"

"I tell you everything anyway."

"That's true." Tiffany and Stephanie had always shared everything with each other. Until now. She hadn't told Tiffany that she'd slept with Geoff.

She grabbed her sister's phone and looked at the message, ready to read it to Tiffany. Did you see this? Beneath the words was a picture of Stephanie and Geoff kissing under the mistletoe at the convention center and a short online article.

"What?" she yelped, dropping the phone. It was a good thing that she was sitting down because she suddenly felt light-headed.

"What's wrong?"

Stephanie couldn't answer so she just shook her head and handed over the phone.

Tiffany took it gingerly, careful not to smear her polish, looked at the message and then laughed. Clearly she saw humor in a situation that wasn't remotely funny. "Oh. You got caught making out with the *not* boyfriend at the rodeo. What were you thinking? As if I didn't know."

"I wasn't thinking that anyone was taking my picture, that's for sure." At least not while they'd been kissing. After, she'd noticed the people with their phones and the photographers, but by then it had been too late.

"Really? Kissing your rodeo rider boyfriend? At a rodeo? In a stadium filled with his fans? And in a world where everyone has a camera?"

"I know. That was stupid."

"No, it wasn't. You were enjoying yourself. You're not used to being photographed everywhere you go. That's not your regular life and it'll take time to get used to it."

"But do I want to get used to it? I don't want people following me around forever."

Tiffany looked at Stephanie, a smile growing on her face. "Are you thinking about forever? Wow. You've just met the man."

"That's not what I meant. We're just having fun. Besides, thinking about forever would be ridiculous, don't you think?"

Tiffany shrugged and laughed ruefully. "You're asking me? I'm no expert on relationships. But I will remind you that Brittany and Daniel fell in love and got married really fast. And they're very happy."

"I wasn't talking about marriage. I'm not even thinking about that." Was she? If not, what type of relationship did she foresee? Geoff was gone a lot so a traditional relationship was out of the question.

"Then what are you thinking?" Tiffany asked as if she'd read her mind.

"I don't know."

"Well, you have time to figure it out, I guess. Unless he proposes soon."

Stephanie laughed. "I don't think I need to worry about that." Geoff had been very clear about what he wanted. A holiday affair. "Let me see your phone again."

"Why?"

"I want to know how many people have seen that picture."

Tiffany glanced at her phone. "Oh."

That didn't sound good. "What?"

"It's gone viral. Like it or not, you're going to be famous for kissing Geoff Burris."

Stephanie closed her eyes, wondering how one fleeting moment could disrupt her entire life. How would Geoff feel about the picture? It definitely would give the impression that the two of them were involved. She'd find out soon enough.

"I hadn't even considered that."

"Looking at the clinch, that much is obvious." Tiffany laughed. "You know what I say. Live your life and don't worry about what anyone else thinks. You don't know these people anyway. And you certainly can't go back and change anything. And if you could, would you?"

That question was easy to answer. "No." She'd enjoyed herself with Geoff. "Are your nails dry? Because I'm ready to go."

Tiffany held out her hands, studying her manicure. "Yep. Let's get out of here."

After they paid for their service, adding generous tips, they got into their cars and went their separate ways. Once Stephanie was home, she grabbed a quick bite to eat and then got ready for the rodeo. She'd skipped the morning events where people could buy tickets to see the bulls, broncos and calves. She didn't feel the desire to get up close and personal with the animals. Not that she thought it was like a petting zoo. Still, if she wanted to be around animals, which she didn't, she could visit her friend Daphne's animal rescue.

Since this was the last day of the rodeo, she expected the convention center to be overflowing with people. As time for the main event grew nearer, she grew more excited. She was practically vibrating as she entered the arena and found her seat. Though last night she'd enjoyed the VIP treatment—the food had been fabulous and his parents were great—she'd felt a little bit removed from the action so tonight she was going to sit with the crowd. Their energy had been off the charts and she wanted to be a part of that. She hadn't been able to convince Tiffany to attend with her, but her brothers, Ethan and Lucas, had taken Geoff up on his offer for tickets. They arrived with their dates soon after she did, and they talked until the lights dimmed.

Her heart sped up with anticipation as a hush went over the crowd. Then the spotlight appeared in the center of the ring, illuminating Geoff, and her heart began to race for an entirely different reason. He looked so good in his jeans, plaid shirt and black cowboy hat that her mouth began to water. She managed to tear her eyes away from Geoff and caught Lucas staring at her, a smirk on his face. *Great.* There would be even more ribbing in her future. He and Ethan had already teased her about the viral picture of her and Geoff kissing. It seemed every person in the United States had seen that photo. Every person except her parents, she hoped.

She rolled her eyes at her brother and then turned her attention back to Geoff. Once he started to speak, everyone and everything vanished. It was as if they were the only two people in the world. She leaned forward, her elbows on her knees, as his voice wrapped around her, welcoming her to the final day of the Mistletoe Rodeo. Then the event started. As the night progressed, Stephanie found herself standing on her feet clapping and cheering loudly for each participant. She held her breath whenever Geoff's brothers competed, only leaning back in her chair once each was done.

Lucas elbowed her and shook his head. "How are you going to stand watching Geoff ride if just watching his brothers makes you this nervous?"

She didn't have an answer to that question. Lucas must not have expected one since he turned back to the ring to watch the next rider.

Finally the last competitor had ridden and trophies had been awarded. Ross and Jack had won their competitions and Mike had come in second in his. There was only one person left. *Geoff.* After his injury, he hadn't been in top form, so he had pulled out of the competition. Not wanting to disappoint his fans, he'd still decided to ride.

A man's voice filled the arena, excitement in his every word. "And now, the moment we've all been waiting for. The son of Bronco himself. The biggest star in rodeo. Ladies and gentlemen, put your hands together and give a Bronco welcome to the one and only Geoff Burris."

The roar of the crowd was deafening, yet Stephanie could hear her heart thudding in her chest. Geoff was still under a doctor's care and hadn't been released to participate. He could injure himself even more. Why was he taking such a chance? Though it was foolish and superstitious, her mind immediately went back to the haunted bar stool at Doug's place. Geoff had sat there. Would he become yet another casualty?

Frowning and calling herself all kinds of ridiculous for even entertaining the notion, she shook the thought away. And then, though it was equally superstitious and foolish, she crossed her fingers and wished for good luck.

Then Geoff burst into the ring on the back of a bucking bronco. Stephanie's heart was in her throat the entire time he was performing, and she wasn't certain she'd even breathed. The horse jumped and spun, but somehow Geoff managed to hang on. And then just that quickly, it was over. Geoff jumped from the horse's back and tossed his hat into the air. It took a moment before she realized she was on her feet, clapping and cheering right along with everyone else. The nurse in her might be annoyed with the risk he'd taken, but the woman in her was proud of the way he'd performed. She knew how much it meant to him. Judging from the prolonged standing ovation, it meant a lot to the fans, too.

"Wow," Lucas said. "That was something else. I can't believe that he had surgery a couple of weeks ago."

"I know."

The lights turned on, signaling the end of the show. The applause gradually slowed and eventually stopped as people began putting on their coats and gathering their belongings. Stephanie did the same. The rodeo had officially come to an end so the audience would be leaving the conference center. Hopefully that would make it easier for Stephanie to reach the backstage area.

She said goodbye to her brothers and their dates and then walked to the backstage door. After giving her name to the guard, she went in search of Geoff. A great number of the contestants had already left so it was relatively easy to spot him. He and his brothers were standing together, talking and laughing, and Stephanie stood back and watched their interaction. She came from a close family and it made her happy to see that despite their differences, they had that in common.

Geoff saw her and waved her over. When she reached them, he draped his good arm around her shoulders and kissed her cheek. Although the kiss was chaste, tingles danced up and down her spine and she fought to keep from revealing just how much his touch affected her. She'd gotten along well with his brothers and had a feeling that if her knees wobbled even a little bit, they'd tease her as mercilessly as her own brothers would.

"I'm Jack." Geoff's brother reached out his hand, and she shook it.

"I'm sorry," Geoff said. "Stephanie, this is my brother, Jack. Jack, this is Stephanie."

"Nice to meet you," Stephanie said, smiling. He was just as handsome as the other Burris brothers. When he smiled, he had a mischievous glint in his eyes. In that second she knew she would like him as much as she liked Mike and Ross.

"Likewise."

Geoff looked around as if making sure that they hadn't forgotten anything and then picked up his duffel. Immediately, Mike took it from him and slung it over his own shoulder. "I got that."

Before Geoff could object, Mike walked away, Ross and Jack beside him.

"They're just looking out for you," Stephanie said.

"I'm fine. I don't need them looking out for me. Didn't you see me ride?"

"I did. And I have to admit that I was a bit worried about you."

"Needlessly."

"Obviously," she said. "You were great."

He faked shock. "What did you say?"

"Please don't make me repeat it."

He laughed as he took her hand. They walked

side by side to the parking lot. He walked her to her car and then leaned against the hood. "Meet you at your place?"

"Yes."

He kissed her briefly and then opened her car door for her, waiting until she'd started the motor before walking away. As Stephanie drove away, her anticipation increased. She couldn't wait to be alone with Geoff again. It was the part of the night she was most looking forward to.

Geoff rolled over and reached across the bed, encountering only the cool sheet and pillow. Sighing, he opened his eyes. It was still dark outside and he hoped that Stephanie would return to bed. The sound of the shower quickly squashed that hope. She'd told him last night that she had to work today. He respected the job she did as a nurse and was so proud of her. Still, he wished they could spend more time together.

Throwing off the warm blankets, he hopped into his pants, pulled on his shirt and then automatically made the bed before leaving the room. He went into the kitchen and pulled a package of bacon from the refrigerator and a loaf of bread from the pantry, then started the coffeemaker. He might not have full use of his arm yet, but he could microwave bacon and make toast. He was just putting a plate on the table when Stephanie breezed into the kitchen, smelling and looking like heaven.

"Wow. You cooked for me. Thanks."

"It's not much, but now that I have a little more use of my arm, I'm able to do some things again."

Her eyes narrowed. "About usage of that arm…"

"I know what you're going to say. You think that I shouldn't have ridden last night. Let's not have that conversation."

She closed the distance between them, pressing against him, and his body immediately jumped to attention. "Actually, I was going to say that you've proven that you're one hundred per cent healed. At least in my estimation. And I'm not talking about the rodeo."

He smiled as he caught her meaning. "Oh."

She sat down and started to eat. He joined her and sipped his coffee.

"You aren't eating?"

"No. I'm not much for breakfast."

"It's the most important meal of the day."

He swiped a piece of bacon from her plate and took a bite. "What are you doing for Thanksgiving?"

"Going to my parents'. What about you?"

"Same. This is the first time in years that we'll all be home for the holidays. Needless to say my mother is thrilled."

"I bet."

"But I want to spend the day with you."

"You're more than welcome to join us for dinner if your parents wouldn't mind."

"They'll be okay with it if I tell them I'm having dinner with you." In fact, he was certain his mother would be overjoyed. "How would you feel about joining my family for dessert? They really liked you and I know they'd like to get to know you better."

"That would be nice. I'd like that." She swallowed the last of her coffee and then stood. "I need to get out of here in a few minutes."

He cleaned the kitchen and was standing by the front door when she was ready to go to work. Kissing her goodbye, he headed for home and was just stepping inside his parents' living room when his phone rang.

"Have you seen the news?" Geoff's agent's voice was loud and he pulled the phone away from his ear. Geoff couldn't tell whether the man was happily excited or upset. Troy was a great agent, but he tended to speak loudly unless he was perfectly calm, which wasn't often.

"No. What's up?"

"You're trending all over social media. All of the sports shows are talking about your ride last night. I've never seen anything like it. Especially for rodeo. I just got a call from a talk show in LA. They want to book you for the day before Thanksgiving. You'll fly out early Wednesday and fly home Thanksgiving morning."

"What? Travel on Thanksgiving? I have plans. Can't we move it back a week or so?"

"This is a big deal, Geoff. Huge. You can't say no. Thanksgiving is three days away as it is. And a week is a lifetime in show business. In another week people might not even remember your ride. We need to strike while the iron is hot. This is the opportunity to inform people about rodeo's diverse history. That is one of your goals, right?"

"Yeah."

It wasn't a difficult decision to make. He'd do the interview. Especially if he'd be back in time for dinner with Stephanie's family. "Okay. I'll do it."

After getting the details, Geoff hung up. He had a busy day ahead of him. Although he wanted to call Stephanie and share his good news, he didn't have time.

He spent all of the morning and a good deal of the afternoon shooting promotional spots for Taylor Beef. He'd done commercials for other products in the past and he was still amazed by how long it took to film a thirty- or sixty-second commercial. He liked being active and the amount of downtime on the set was a bit unnerving.

Geoff must have repeated his lines a hundred times before the director was satisfied with the result. Though he'd done nothing more strenuous than hold up a steak, Geoff was worn out. Probably from fighting off boredom.

When he'd fulfilled his obligation, he went home. His parents were still at work and none of his brothers were around so he heated up some leftovers and then decided to take advantage of his privacy and call Stephanie. She was really busy and only had a few minutes to talk. She told him she didn't have to work tomorrow so he quickly invited her out for the day and she accepted.

"Wear jeans. And boots."

"I assume you don't mean fashion boots."

He laughed. Although he found her colorful boots sexy as hell, that wasn't what he'd meant. "No. Do you have a pair of basic cowboy boots?"

"I don't own *basic* anything. Or hadn't you noticed?"

Oh, he'd noticed all right. There was nothing basic about Stephanie Brandt.

"But I can borrow a pair from my sister, Brittany," Stephanie continued. "We wear the same size shoes and she's married to a horse rancher so I'm sure she has an extra pair." She faked a sigh. "I guess I can endure wearing plain boots for a few hours."

"I appreciate your sacrifice. Does eleven work for you?"

"Yep." He could hear conversation in the background and knew she needed to get back to work.

"Okay then, see you in the morning."

"Bye."

Once he'd ended the call, he put the rest of his plans into motion. He was taking a big step with Stephanie. But since his feelings were growing with each passing day, he didn't feel the need to try and control them. At least not yet.

Chapter Ten

"Where are we going?" Stephanie asked as Geoff drove away from Bronco and toward the highway.

"A ranch."

"I gathered that much when you asked me to wear these boots." Stephanie frowned at the plain brown boots. They were so not her style. Brittany had teased her, saying she must really like Geoff if she were going to dress down for the day. Then, before Stephanie could reply, Brittany had mentioned the viral picture of the kiss. Sisters could be as bad as brothers when it came to teasing. But unlike with Lucas or Ethan, Stephanie couldn't punch her sister in the arm.

"It's the ranch where I learned to ride," Geoff replied.

"Really?"

"Yes. It's a place that means a lot to me."

"How did you get into rodeo?" She turned in her seat to look at him. "I know you told me about going to a rodeo when you were a kid, but what made you stick with it?"

He smiled and her stomach lurched. She'd been around him for a while, and they'd been intimate, yet whenever they were alone together, she felt as if she was floating on air. True, their relationship was still new, but she had a sneaking suspicion that she'd still be getting this feeling forty years from now.

That thought brought her up short and she struggled to grab ahold of herself. She didn't want to be one of those women who jumped into the deep end of the relationship pool, convincing herself that the man felt the same way as she did. Doing so would only leave her vulnerable to heartbreak. Just because she was in danger of falling in love with Geoff didn't mean he felt the same. He might just be having a good time. As far as he knew, that was what she was doing, too.

"I can't explain it. Something about it appealed to me on a basic level. I was young, so I can't say that it was as if I knew this was my life's calling, but it was as close to that as possible for a kid. And then I wanted to learn more about Black rodeo riders. There's history there, but it's not widely known. Bill Pickett and Nat Love were superstars in their eras. Legends."

"And now there's you."

"I don't put myself in their category. I'm just doing my best to honor them and try to follow in their footsteps."

She didn't doubt for a moment his sincerity. He was truly humble and wanted to do his best to live up to the greats who hadn't had the same opportunities he'd been granted. "You're doing a wonderful job. I saw the expressions on the faces of lots of boys and girls at the Mistletoe Rodeo. You're an inspiration to them."

"That's why it was so important for me to ride. I know a lot of those kids had come just to see me. I didn't want anyone to go home disappointed."

"Luckily it all worked out."

He winked at her. "There was no luck involved. It was all skill."

She shook her head and laughed.

They neared a mailbox, and he slowed the car, turning into a wide gravel driveway. When they reached a large house with deep porches, Geoff parked and then turned off the engine.

Stephanie looked around. With its enormous lawn surrounded by a white picket fence, the ranch looked idyllic.

As she and Geoff got out of his car, the front door opened and a smiling middle-aged woman stepped onto the porch. She was wearing jeans, boots and a thick gray sweater. She waved them inside. "Come on in where it's warm."

Geoff led Stephanie up the wide stairs. Although it was cold, Stephanie took a moment to admire the Christmas decorations. Colorful lights had been strung on the enormous evergreen tree in the center of the yard. Lights were strung along the front porch and down the banisters and covered the evergreen bushes that ran the width of the house. Stephanie imagined it looked quite festive at night.

Once they were inside, the woman hugged Geoff and then turned and smiled at Stephanie. "You must be Stephanie. I'm Nancy Trotter. It's nice to meet you."

"You, too."

"Come on into the living room. There's a nice fire going." Nancy gestured to a room to the right of the foyer where a huge stone fireplace dominated one wall of the two-story space. "I made a pot of coffee and frosted the cake. I just need to get the cookies out of the oven. Make yourselves comfortable. Hank will be along in a minute."

They sat in the cozy seating area around the fireplace. A moment later, Nancy returned, carrying the refreshments. Geoff jumped up and immediately took the tray from her.

"It's not that heavy," she said even as she relinquished the tray. "Besides, didn't you just have surgery?"

"Even so, my mother would tan my hide if I just sat here instead of helping."

"Your mother never laid a hand on you a day in your life and you know it."

"No, but she'd never let me hear the end of it, which is worse."

Nancy laughed, then poured them each some coffee and offered them the homemade sweets.

Stephanie was in the middle of sipping her warm drink when Nancy looked at her over her own coffee mug. "So, Geoff tells me you're a nurse."

Geoff laughed. "Yes, she's a nurse. Please don't give Stephanie the third degree."

"I'm just making conversation," the older woman said innocently.

Stephanie wondered briefly if Nancy questioned all the women Geoff brought to the ranch. And just how many women had come before her? She pushed the thought out of her mind. It really didn't matter. She laid a hand on Geoff's and turned to Nancy. "Yes, I'm a nurse. That's actually how Geoff and I met."

"Nursing is a great calling. And definitely necessary as long as men insist on riding bulls and other such nonsense."

Stephanie smiled. She had a feeling she and Nancy had more in common than it first appeared. Though the woman had to be in her midfifties, her eyes twinkled with mischief. She obviously had a great sense of humor. More importantly, she didn't treat Geoff like he was a big star, something Stephanie knew he appreciated. He looked relaxed and at home.

Before Geoff could comment, a man who Stephanie presumed was Hank lumbered in. He was a mountain of a man, well over six feet. He had a full head of gray hair and had to be in his late fifties or early sixties, but he looked as strong as an ox. "Welcome, Geoff. Good to see you."

Geoff and the other man hugged, and then Geoff introduced him to Stephanie.

"I want to show Stephanie where I first learned to ride."

Hank's dark brown eyes lit up and he gave a hearty laugh as he turned to Stephanie. "Those were the days. I have never seen a more determined or stubborn rider than Geoff. He insisted that he was ready to ride the toughest and most rank broncos. He spent more time sitting in the dirt than anything else. But he kept coming back."

Geoff laughed. "I was younger then. And foolish. Luckily little kids bounce."

"The stories I could tell you," Hank said, grinning broadly.

"Now, Hank, don't go and do that," Nancy said. "Geoff's never brought a woman to meet us before. You need to be on your best behavior so he'll bring her back."

Stephanie's heart leaped at the other woman's words. Stephanie wasn't one of a long line of women Geoff had brought to the Trotter ranch. She was the only one. What did that mean? Was she as special to him as he was becoming to her? Or maybe it was simply a matter of him not being in Bronco often.

"I'd love to hear the stories," Stephanie said.

"Oh, no." Geoff jumped to his feet, setting his empty mug and dessert plate on the tray. "What I'd really like to do is show Stephanie around the ranch."

"Go right ahead," Hank said, then grinned at Geoff. "We'll be here when you're done."

Stephanie stood and took the hand Geoff offered her. They put on their coats and went around the back of the house. Decorative reindeer pulling Santa's sleigh filled the side lawn, extending the Christmas spirit to this part of the property, as well. When they reached the backyard, Stephanie looked around. In the distance she spotted barns and corrals.

"This is nice. And huge."

"I spent all my free time here as a boy. I practically lived here. Hank and Nancy are like my second parents."

"They clearly love you."

He grinned and pulled her closer to him, giving her a quick kiss on her cheek. "What's not to love? Am I right?"

She shook her head. "I think your ego is big enough. I won't be adding to it."

"Tough crowd." He tugged her hand. "Let me show you around."

Stephanie nodded and followed him across the snowy ground to one of the corrals. A few horses wearing blankets milled about, nosing each other. One horse snorted and took off running. The corral fence went long past what Stephanie could see, giving the horse plenty of space to roam.

Stephanie leaned against the corral fence and hooked one foot over the bottom rail. "This ranch is beautiful."

"It's one of my favorite places. There's something freeing about ranch living. You can breathe. And it's quiet enough that you can actually hear yourself think."

"Unlike Bronco, that bustling metropolis," Stephanie quipped.

"I know Bronco isn't all that big. And it certainly isn't overpopulated by any means."

"I was kidding. I know you spend most of your time on the road. I guess the rodeo life is busier than I thought."

"Yes. I don't have a lot of quiet time to myself. Not that I'm complaining."

"You don't have to tell me that. I understand that you're describing your life to me. It doesn't make you ungrateful if you don't pretend like everything is roses and champagne."

He gave her an appreciative glance. "One day, when my career is over, I want a ranch of my own."

"That sounds nice."

"I think so. I wanted to buy a ranch for my parents, but they like living in town. Since they both work there and neither one of them is talking about retiring anytime soon, it makes sense for them to stay there."

"They like their home."

"Yeah. I wanted to get them a newer place in Bronco Heights, but they said they were perfectly happy living in the house where we'd grown up."

"The house must be filled with memories."

He nodded. "And to be honest, I like returning there whenever I can and sleeping in my old room."

She turned an assessing gaze his way. "I didn't take you for the sentimental type."

"You think I'm being sentimental?"

She shrugged. "You must have created memories here, too."

"Yes. And I'd like to make a couple more. With you."

He closed the distance between them and cupped her face with his calloused hand. Then in the space it took for her to inhale, he leaned down and kissed her lips. His touch was gentle and yet it aroused desires in her. Geoff could take her from zero to lusting in under a second.

She wrapped her arms around his neck and pressed closer to him. His muscles were rock-hard and she loved the way they felt against her softer body. Nothing in her past experiences had prepared her for Geoff. He had a way of awakening her body, teasing it into burning desire. After a moment, he pulled away, leaning his forehead against hers. Neither of them spoke while they tried to get their breathing under control.

After a moment, he took her hand and they continued their tour of the ranch. They walked a short distance and they stopped beside a tree. She looked at him quizzically. "What's special about this tree?"

"It's where I used to sit and eat a snack when Hank forced me to take a break. I used to climb up to sit on the branches and look across the ranch while I ate, counting the seconds until I could ride again."

He pointed to a fenced-in area. "And that is where I managed to stay on a bronco's back for eight seconds. After that, you couldn't tell me nothing. I knew I was ready for the big time."

Stephanie laughed. She knew he was sharing more than memories with her. He was sharing *himself* with her. Letting her see a side of him that the general public never saw. She knew he shared his life with his fans, but he held parts of himself back, keeping it for those who mattered most to him.

Stephanie was happy to be in that number.

After about ninety minutes, they returned to the house. Geoff knocked on the door and they stepped inside.

"We're in the kitchen," Nancy called.

Stephanie followed Geoff through the house, looking around. The old-fashioned furniture gleamed and the rooms smelled vaguely of lemon furniture wax.

"I just wanted to say goodbye before we leave," Geoff said.

"It was so good to see you," Nancy said as she and Hank hugged each of them. "And, Stephanie, feel free to come on out and visit anytime."

"I just might do that."

The Trotters walked them through the house, following them onto the porch.

Once they were in the car and driving back to Bronco, Stephanie turned to Geoff. "Thanks for bringing me here. I had a really good time."

"Thanks for coming with me."

As they drove down the highway, Stephanie thought that their relationship had just taken a step toward becoming more serious. At least her feelings were becoming deeper. The thought didn't worry her as much as she would have thought. Perhaps because she was coming to believe that she was as special to Geoff as he was to her.

Geoff glanced over at Stephanie. It was late afternoon and the sun would be setting soon. Even in the fading light, she was absolutely stunning. He'd never met a more beautiful woman. But that physical beauty paled when compared to her inner beauty. He thought of how friendly she'd been to Nancy and Hank and of the way she'd gotten along with his brothers. His parents had raved about her after they'd watched the rodeo together. All in all, she'd won over his family and those closest to him.

And then there was the way she treated him. While other women he'd dated had been impressed by his fame and fortune, Stephanie cared about him and his well-being. His money didn't matter to her. Although he hadn't mentioned it to her, he appreciated the way she worried about his health. She was more concerned about his recovery than she was about him continuing to shine in front of crowds. He might not have agreed with her position, but he did like the way she cared. And she definitely wasn't trying to share his spotlight.

On the way home they stopped at a local grocery store and picked up a rotisserie chicken, sides and a bagged salad. While they were standing in the checkout line, Geoff spotted a tabloid magazine with a picture of him on the cover. The headline mentioned the Mistletoe Rodeo, so he put the magazine on the conveyer belt. Hopefully the article was filled with good reviews about the rodeo.

Once they got to Stephanie's house, she excused herself to change her clothes. While he waited, he opened the magazine, looking for the article about the rodeo.

To his shock, beside the article about the rodeo was a picture of Stephanie with a caption that nearly stole his breath: GOLD DIGGER? As he scanned the article, his anger grew with each word he read, and by the time he reached the last paragraph, he was enraged. One of Stephanie's former boyfriends claimed that she was dating Geoff because she was after his money, something he alleged she had a habit of doing.

How dared they print such garbage about Stephanie? She wasn't a celebrity used to being subjected to such lies. She was a private person. On more than one occasion, she'd pointed out that she liked living outside of the limelight. Geoff respected that and tried to shield her from unwanted attention. It wasn't always possible, but most of the time, he'd been successful.

But more than invading her privacy, the paper had printed lies. Anyone who knew Stephanie knew that money didn't matter to her. Sure, she wanted to be compensated fairly for her labor as well she should, but cash wasn't the be-all and end-all for her. She appreciated the small things, like hanging out with his friends at a dive bar or grabbing ribs with his brothers. Having spa days with her sister and dinner with her family. He knew that. But what about the people who didn't know her? Potential patients who might not trust her because of the lies the paper had printed.

Stephanie came back into the room. She'd changed out of her boots and jeans and was now wearing pink sweats and fuzzy house shoes. She'd been talking when she entered the room, but after taking one look at him, she froze. Gasped. "What's wrong?"

"What do you mean?"

"You don't look like yourself. You look…angry. And you haven't answered my question, so I'll ask it again. What's wrong?"

He briefly considered not telling her what he'd read, but dismissed the idea immediately. He didn't want to lie to her. Honesty was an important part of every relationship. Besides, he knew all about rumors. They didn't go away just because you wished they would. They lingered for days, often weeks, until another juicy piece of gossip replaced them. She was bound to hear it, and it was better if she heard it from him.

He held out his hand, beckoning her closer. "Come here."

She slowly crossed the room, dread written all over her beautiful face. She was holding her breath as if waiting for him to tell her something horrible. Seeing her fear, he couldn't force himself to say the words, so he handed her the newspaper. Unable to sit still while she read the poison printed on the page, he paced back and forth, trying to rein in his anger. She set down the paper and stared into space. When he saw the destroyed look on her face, his fury reignited.

"It's not true," she said softly. "I'm not some gold digger."

"I never for a second thought you were."

"The guy they quoted is an ex-boyfriend of mine. We dated for a few months. But that was years ago, when I was getting my nursing degree. It didn't work out. And it's true that I dated a surgeon after we broke up, but not because I was looking for someone with money like he claims. I'm a nurse. I work in a hospital. I meet lots of doctors. Some of them are nice. And I dated a couple. But that was before I established my no dating coworkers policy."

He knelt in front of her chair, gently grabbing her hands. "You don't have to explain anything to me. I know the kind of person you are. I know that you're not after me for my money."

She looked at him. She must have seen the truth in his eyes because she nodded. Smiled. Then her smile faded and her brow wrinkled. "I just don't understand. I haven't dated Aaron in years. I haven't even seen him. How did this reporter even find him? And why would anyone bother digging into my past? And why would they print this story without even talking to me first to find out if what he said was true?"

"I don't know the answers to all of your questions, but I know the answer to one. They dug into your past because of me."

"You?"

He nodded. "Your connection to me. I have a great relationship with most sports reporters. I respect them and they respect me and my privacy. They would never consider digging into your life. But the person who wrote this? I've never met her. Until I read her name on the byline, I'd never even heard of her. Obviously she's trying to make a name for herself."

"By dragging mine through the mud?"

"Sadly, yes. And to be honest, I have no idea how she and your ex-boyfriend connected. Maybe he reached out to her."

She frowned. "It doesn't really matter. The deed has been done and the dirt has been spread. I imagine by the end of the day every tabloid in the country will be carrying this story."

"And anyone who knows you will recognize it as the garbage that it is."

"And people who don't know me? The patients I treat? My coworkers? People that I pass on the street in Bronco? All of them could read this article."

Regret left a bad taste in his mouth. "I'm so sorry, Stephanie. I wish there was something I could do to make this all go away."

"What will your family think? They don't know me very well."

"They haven't known you for very long, but they know you well enough. They like you. They aren't going to let some third-rate rag change that. To be honest, I wouldn't care if they'd printed something about me. I just don't like them bringing you into this. I hate that they're making you upset." Seeing the sad look on her face was more than he could bear. It was like a knife to the heart.

She stiffened her shoulders. "I'm not going to let it bother me. Aaron has been out of my life for years. He's not getting back in. And do I care if people who don't know me and who I don't know think I'm a gold digger? No."

He kissed her lips. "That's my girl." Though he didn't press her, he knew she was lying, something totally out of character for her. He knew it would hurt her deeply if people got the wrong impression about her. He hated that his fame was coming between them, especially since it was causing her pain. Hopefully this would be the first and last article about her. "Let's go eat."

Stephanie nodded, but he could tell her heart wasn't in it. Some way or another he was going to make this up to her.

He just wished he knew how.

Chapter Eleven

The next morning, Stephanie walked into the hospital, holding her head up as high as she could. She knew her friends and coworkers wouldn't believe the trash that tabloid had printed, but even so, a part of her still dreaded facing them. She would rather have stayed home and waited for it to blow over, but she also knew that avoiding the problem wouldn't get rid of it. Sooner or later she'd have to face everyone. Might as well get it over with now.

"Hey," Tamara said as Stephanie entered the nurses' lounge. Several others were in there getting ready for their shifts and they looked up.

"Morning," Stephanie replied. But instead of meeting her coworkers' eyes she twisted the lock on her locker and then jerked on the handle. The door didn't open so she entered the combination again, focusing on getting each number correct before moving to the next.

"Nobody believes a word in that article." The voice behind her made Stephanie turn around. Surprisingly it was Lisa who stood there giving her that reassurance. If anyone would have taken the opportunity to get in a dig, Stephanie would have thought it would be her. But then Stephanie had heard that Lisa and Dr. Williamson had gone on a few dates. Maybe now that she didn't view Stephanie as a romantic rival, she was willing to be cordial.

Stephanie looked around at the other nurses. They all nodded in agreement.

"Don't worry." Tamara spoke up. "If someone makes a snide remark to you, or even looks at you wrong, let us know. We'll handle it."

That sounded ominous. Especially so coming from Tamara who was not quite five feet and maybe weighed a hundred pounds holding a ten-pound dumbbell.

"Thanks," Stephanie said. "I knew none of you would believe any of that story, but I'm still a little bit embarrassed."

"You shouldn't be," Tamara said. "If anyone should be embarrassed it's your ex-boyfriend. What kind of man wants the entire world to know that he's a bum who lost the best thing that ever happened to him?"

"I wouldn't say I was all that," Stephanie said. "We didn't date all that long."

"Work with me here," Tamara said, and they all laughed. "I prefer my version."

"It's your story so tell it your way," Stephanie said, as she put her coat and scarf into the locker.

She changed into her nursing shoes, shoved her boots into her locker and slammed the door. As far as she was concerned, she was closing the door on the gossip, too. She'd been knocked off balance for a minute, but she was back on center. She didn't think anyone would mention the article to her, but if they did, she wouldn't need anyone to defend her. She had four siblings. She knew how to give as good as she got.

Fortunately, nothing untoward happened, and as the hours passed, she began to fully relax. She and Geoff had reservations to go to DJ's Deluxe for dinner and she was looking forward to their date. With Geoff by her side, she knew she might draw attention, but being with him was worth it. Having people watch her might not be her favorite thing in the world, but eventually they would get tired of looking at her. At least she hoped it worked out that way. Luckily, she didn't have many ex-boyfriends, so the gossip reporters wouldn't be able to mine her past for more stories.

She decided a red knit dress and boots would be perfect for tonight. She was running a comb through her hair when her doorbell rang. Geoff. She hurried to the door and let him in. He closed the door and then swept her into a deep kiss that sent all of her concerns sailing out the window. Everything was right with the world when they were together.

Her heart was pounding when he released her and she wobbled. Laughing, he put his arm around her waist and tugged her against his chest so she could lean on him. "I don't see how you can walk on those skinny high heels."

Stephanie hadn't lost her balance because of the boots. She'd been wearing high heels ever since she'd been a fashion-loving teenager. His kiss had been the reason. Of course she wasn't going to tell him that he'd practically made her swoon. A woman needed a few secrets. Especially since he hadn't been knocked off-kilter when they'd kissed. Not that she believed he'd been unaffected. She could tell by the way he surreptitiously wiped his hand across his forehead that he had been.

"Oh, I manage."

"What do you do when there's snow and ice on the ground? Wearing them then would be dangerous."

"Says the man whose job involves riding on the back of a bucking animal."

"It's not the same thing at all."

"Well, if I find myself slipping, I'll grab ahold of your arm. How's that?"

"You don't need to be falling to do that. Feel free to grab my arm or anything else whenever the spirit moves you."

"Don't tempt me." She put on her coat and scarf and then took Geoff's outstretched hand as they left.

A few minutes later, when they were being seated at the restaurant, they only got a few looks and stares from people taken by Geoff's celebrity. Fortunately the crowd in DJ's Deluxe were locals who'd grown used to seeing Geoff around town. Other than a quick hello, they hadn't made a big deal out of his presence and Stephanie and Geoff were able to enjoy their meal in peace. Even better, nobody gave Stephanie a second glance. Either they hadn't heard about her ex-boyfriend's lies, or they hadn't given them any credence. Whatever the reason, it worked for Stephanie. Everything was right in the world again and she was glad she'd shown her face in public. Now she knew that the gossip had been put to rest.

After dinner, they returned to Stephanie's house. Even though they hadn't been dating long, she'd grown used to having him around. He was easy to be with and she enjoyed their cozy relationship. He seemed comfortable in her home.

"Want some hot chocolate?" Geoff asked as soon as they stepped inside.

"You already know the answer to that," she said, heading for her bedroom. "I'm going to change. You know your way around my kitchen." She had a pair of warm sweats waiting for her. The snow was beautiful and she loved a white Christmas, but she would be so glad when spring arrived and the weather warmed up. Of course spring was still months away.

Even though she was putting on sweats, she still wanted to look cute. The ones she chose weren't baggy but rather hugged her curves. She checked her appearance in the mirror and then, pleased by what she saw, blew a kiss to her reflection. When she returned to the living room, their drinks were on the coffee table. Geoff was sitting on the couch, staring at the TV. He glanced up at her but didn't smile. Instead he turned back to the television.

"What's wrong?"

He shook his head. Sitting down, she looked at the screen. One of those celebrity gossip shows was on. For a horrible moment, she thought the announcer was talking about her, repeating the lies that her ex-boyfriend and that so-called reporter had spread about her. Happily, she wasn't the topic of this discussion and she blew out a breath. But her relief was short-lived. The announcer was introducing one of Geoff's former girlfriends who was giving an exclusive interview.

The camera switched to a perfectly made-up woman who was so beautiful she could have been on the cover of a magazine. She tearfully recounted her relationship with Geoff. According to her, Geoff had promised her the world, claiming that he wanted to build a life with her. She'd fallen madly in love with him and been blindsided when he dumped her out of the blue. He hadn't even given her a reason.

"Why are you coming forward now?" the interviewer asked.

"Because I want to deliver a message." The camera moved in for a close-up and the woman stared straight into it. "Stephanie, you seem like a nice person. Run, don't walk away from Geoff before he breaks your heart the way he broke mine."

Geoff clicked the remote, muting the program. "That's a crock and she knows it."

Stephanie waited for him to elaborate. When he only sat there glowering at the TV, she turned to him. "So what did happen?"

Stephanie knew there were two sides to every story and Geoff's version could be a lot different. But even so, her mama didn't raise a fool. She needed for Geoff to do more than scowl at the TV. He had to tell her something. She wanted him to say that he cared for her more than he'd ever cared for his ex-girlfriend or any of the women he'd dated.

She hated being insecure, but she wasn't going to ignore what she'd just seen and heard, especially since they hadn't ever defined their relationship. Geoff hadn't made a secret of the fact that he was only in town for a short while. He'd come specifically for the Mistletoe Rodeo, which was over. If he hadn't been injured, he'd be making plans to rejoin the tour and who knows what that meant for the two of them. Ridiculously, she thought of the haunted bar stool. Perhaps their relationship had been doomed from the beginning.

"I don't want to talk about her."

"What?" He couldn't be serious. He'd seen the same interview she had. Was he really going to leave Stephanie with these unanswered questions?

"I didn't press you about the article with your former boyfriend, did I?"

"No, but that was your decision. If you want to talk about it, we can. I have nothing to hide."

"I don't need to discuss it. You said he was lying and I believe you. I would appreciate the same trust from you."

Stephanie pressed her lips closed. The two situations weren't even remotely the same. Surely he could see that. She didn't want to argue, especially when it was clear that Geoff wasn't going to change his mind. As far as he was concerned, the topic was off-limits. Fine. She wasn't happy about it, but she wasn't going to beg him to talk to her.

She crossed her arms and moved to the far end of the sofa.

"Come on," Geoff said. "Don't be that way."

"I'm not being any way. You don't want to talk so we don't have to talk."

Geoff blew out a breath. "It's not worth it. But Cynthia's version of the past is not how things went down."

"So how did things go down?"

"I told you, it's not worth talking about."

Well, that told her absolutely nothing. Suddenly the atmosphere was filled with tension. The good feeling from earlier was gone and Stephanie didn't know how to get it back. Moreover, she didn't think it was her responsibility to try to restore the good mood. She might not be right, but she definitely wasn't wrong. She needed what she needed.

Maybe Geoff couldn't reassure her. Maybe he didn't understand how insecure she felt in this moment. Or maybe he didn't care enough about her to find out what she needed. In the end, his reason didn't matter.

The haunted bar stool might not be at the root of the problem, but this might be a sign that they should slow things down. Even though she could imagine a future with Geoff, the truth was that they hadn't known each other all that long. Clearly there was more that they needed to learn about each other.

"You know, it's been a long day. I think I'd better get some sleep. I'm off tomorrow and I have a lot of errands to run. You should go now." She stood, ignoring the startled look on Geoff's face. Apparently he was just going to pretend everything was right between them. Either he was used to dealing with fake people or the people he usually hung around were so starstruck that they let him get away with everything. Stephanie wasn't that type of person. She wasn't going to pretend not to be bothered by the situation when she was.

"Are you sure?" He stood slowly, then looked into her face. She easily read the concern in his eyes. She ignored it, just as he'd ignored hers.

"Yes. I'll talk to you tomorrow."

When they reached the door, she moved to open it, but Geoff grabbed her hand, preventing her from turning the doorknob. With his other hand he turned her face to his, tipping her chin so that their eyes met. He seemed to be searching for the right words to say. Apparently they didn't come to him, because he didn't say a word. Instead, he brought his mouth down to hers and gave her a searing kiss that nearly melted her bones.

Her knees wobbled, and she clutched his shoulders in order to keep from sliding to the floor. He wrapped his arms around her waist, pressing her closer to him. The kiss went on and on and desire blazed through Stephanie, rebelling against her sensible nature, but with great effort she forced it down. Her body might have forgotten about the claims Geoff's ex-girlfriend had made, but her mind hadn't. She stepped out of his embrace and opened the door.

"I'll talk to you tomorrow," Geoff said firmly before he stepped outside into the winter night.

Stephanie watched him walk away until the cold wind blew, chilling her. She closed the door and then went directly to her laptop where she immediately did a search on Geoff's former girlfriend. There was a link to the television interview, but she ignored it. She'd seen it already and once was definitely enough.

A part of her felt guilty for trying to find more information about Geoff's previous relationships. It felt a bit like prying into his private life, but she couldn't stop herself from searching. It was as if she'd become addicted or worse, possessed by a need to know.

Was this what Geoff's most devoted fans did? Did they scour the internet, looking for any scrap of information about his life? She'd thought she was becoming a part of his life, but now she felt shut out. At least about his past romances. A half hour later they were as much a mystery to her as they'd been before.

Closing her computer, Stephanie grabbed her mug of now cold cocoa and Geoff's barely touched bottle of beer and went to the kitchen. She dumped their beverages down the drain, ignoring the metaphor for their short relationship, then went to her bedroom. There was no chance she was going to fall asleep tonight, but she needed to put distance between herself and her computer.

Geoff drove home slowly, disappointed at the turn the night had taken. His hand clenched the steering wheel as he thought about the lies and half-truths Cynthia had told. And the reporter had sat there, lapping up her story. No one from the show had bothered to reach out to him to get his side of the story before airing the interview. Not that he would have commented. What happened between him and Cynthia had been between *him and Cynthia*. And Roger. Geoff couldn't leave out the man she'd cheated on him with. And Geoff, fool that he'd been, had missed all of the signs. He'd been so besotted and blinded by Cynthia's beauty that he'd ignored what had been right in front of his face. Cynthia knew that he didn't want his idiocy to become public knowledge so she knew he wouldn't respond.

The truth was, he would rather people believed her lies than get into a public discussion about his personal life. As much as he appreciated his fans, they didn't get to know every detail of his life. The private parts of his life would remain private.

He'd never hurt as badly as he was hurting now. Not because of what Cynthia had said. He no longer cared what she did, as long as she did it far away from him. No, his heart was aching because Stephanie hadn't believed in him. He knew he could tell her about Cynthia, but there would never be enough answers to satisfy her. There would always be one more question. One more lingering doubt. He couldn't make her believe in him. She would have to decide to do that on her own. But that didn't mean he wouldn't try to encourage that trust. He knew it wouldn't come with sweet words but with actions. Sadly, she'd kicked him out before he could show her how much she meant to him. He'd tried to put his feelings into that kiss, but one kiss could never do that.

There was always tomorrow. He just needed to come up with a plan.

Unfortunately, given the big lie Cynthia had told, and how convincing she'd been, it needed to be a great plan.

He stayed up all night, coming up with and discarding plan after plan. Although none of them were perfect, there was one common theme. They all included him and Stephanie spending as much time together as possible. Time apart would allow her doubts to grow and fester and could spell the end of their relationship.

This was the absolute worst time for him to have to go to LA. But it was important that he do so. Which was why he was going to ask Stephanie to accompany him if her schedule allowed.

Hopefully she wouldn't think he was being presumptuous. After all, they hadn't known each other very long. It was a big step, especially so early in their relationship. But they would have time to talk on the plane. Neither of them would be able to walk away if the conversation got tough.

They'd have to confront their issues head-on and hopefully clear the air.

After drinking a cup of coffee to clear his head, he called her. Perhaps they could spend time together after she ran her errands, and he could ask her about going with him to LA. He smiled as he heard her voice.

"Hey. I hope I'm not calling too early. I wanted to catch you before you went out. Are you free for lunch?"

"Sorry," she said, sounding rushed. "A couple of the nurses called in sick and they're shorthanded. I'm going in now, so I'll have to take a rain check. Talk to you later."

She hung up before he could even say goodbye and he wondered if this shift really existed, or if she'd created it in order to avoid him as she'd done once before. He forced down the suspicion, choosing to trust Stephanie. It was bad enough that she didn't trust him. Their relationship wouldn't stand a chance if he succumbed to doubt. If he couldn't see her today, there was always tomorrow.

Unfortunately, that didn't turn out to be the case. The nurses were still sick, so in addition to working her regular shift, she'd had to work even more hours. The telephone calls they had were brief and extremely unsatisfying.

Now as he walked through the airport, he tried once more to reach Stephanie before his plane boarded. He would have liked to talk to her before he left, but obviously that wasn't going to happen. So he did the next best thing. He texted her a quick message and then got on the plane.

He stared out the window at the mountains in the distance. There weren't many other people on the plane so he was able to enjoy the flight in peace. Troy had arranged for a car to drive him to the hotel, so not long after landing he was sitting in the back seat of a sleek limousine. He might have been raised in a small town, but he loved big cities. He loved the energy in the air. The movement. The way that there was always something to do.

Even though he got a rush from cities, he would never settle down in one. Bronco was home and he planned to return there when his rodeo days were over. In the past, when he'd envisioned his future, it had been as a single man, happily living the life of an unattached bachelor. Since he'd met Stephanie, the picture had begun to change, and the life he imagined now included a woman by his side. Not just any woman. A strong yet sweet, stubborn yet forgiving woman. A beautiful woman inside and out. Stephanie Brandt was the woman he wanted sharing that future. He just needed to convince her of that.

Whoa. Where had that thought come from? Was he really willing to alter his life's plan mere weeks after meeting Stephanie? Wasn't this strain in their relationship proof that they needed to take time to get to know each other better? Just look at what happened with Cynthia.

The logical part of his brain urged him to be cautious and take things slow. He nearly laughed out loud at the idea. He was a bronc rider. Hell, he'd just ridden a bronc with a busted shoulder. He'd been born without the caution gene.

When he reached the hotel, he took a quick shower and had an early dinner. He had a few minutes before the car came to drive him to the studio so he grabbed his cell phone and punched in Stephanie's number. She might not be able to talk, but he wanted her to know that he was thinking of her now. To be honest she was always in his thoughts. She was the last person on his mind at night and the first person he thought about when he woke up.

"Hello." Her voice lacked the warmth he'd been used to hearing. Perhaps she was busy. Or tired.

He dropped into a chair. "Hey. How are you?"

"Fine. You just caught me. I'm about to leave work."

"How was your day?"

"Fine. Yours?"

He frowned at the phone. He didn't expect her to go into specifics, but he'd wanted more than a one-word answer before she switched the conversation back to him. "The flight was uneventful. I'm in the hotel waiting for my ride to the studio."

"That sounds nice."

Nice? Could she be any more uninterested? "You're going to watch, aren't you?"

"Of course."

Another pause.

"Are we fighting?" he asked.

"What? Of course not. It's just been a long day and I'm ready to get out of here."

That sounded reasonable, but it didn't sit right with him. Something was going on with her. Unfortunately, before he could get into it, he received a text. His driver had arrived and was waiting to take him to the studio. "Okay, then. Go on home. I'll call you after the show if it's not too late."

"Okay. Good luck."

"I believe the appropriate phrase is break a leg."

She laughed and his spirits lifted. Maybe she *was* just tired. "I'm a nurse. There's no way I'll tell a bronc rider to break a leg. I just can't do it."

His laughter mingled with hers as they ended the call. Then he left his room and got into his second limousine of the day. Normally he wouldn't be nervous about a television interview, but tonight was different. Stephanie would be watching. He just hoped he didn't say the wrong thing.

Chapter Twelve

Stephanie clutched the pillow to her chest as she stared at her television. Geoff's interview would be coming up right after the commercial break. Stephanie didn't know why she was nervous, but she was. Her palms were sweating and her heart was racing as if she'd just run a mile. This was ridiculous. She wasn't the one who was about to talk to the entire nation, or at least those who were awake and watching this program. That dubious honor fell to Geoff. When she'd spoken to him earlier, he'd sounded perfectly relaxed and unbothered. If he wasn't quaking in his cowboy boots, why was she suddenly unable to sit still?

That answer to that question was so easy it was laughable. Because her family and friends were watching the show. Her parents and each of her sisters had invited her over to watch the show with them. She'd turned them down, telling them she would be going to bed right after Geoff's interview. The truth was, she was nervous about what Geoff would say and she didn't want any members of her family watching her watch him.

She set the pillow down, grabbed her hot chocolate and took a sip. The sweet drink soothed her, and the warmth spread from her stomach to the rest of her body. She leaned back against the sofa and took a deep breath.

The commercial break ended and the host returned, telling the audience about Geoff and his unparalleled success in the rodeo. Stephanie turned up the volume to be sure she didn't miss a syllable. When he finished his introduction, the camera panned to Geoff as he walked across the stage and sat in a chair across from the host.

Just looking at Geoff made Stephanie's stomach flutter. He was just so handsome. Dressed in a pristine white shirt with a Western cut that looked so good against his brown skin and showed off his muscular torso and pressed black pants that accentuated his powerful thighs, he was the epitome of a rodeo star. Although his cowboy hat was nowhere to be seen, he was wearing his boots.

The host welcomed Geoff to the show.

"Thanks for the invitation." Although he hadn't said anything out of the ordinary, Stephanie smiled and some of her nerves faded away.

They chatted a bit about Geoff's background and how he'd become interested in rodeo. Stephanie heard the pride in Geoff's voice as he talked about seeing the Bill Pickett Invitational Rodeo as a boy and the impact it had on his life. He then mentioned Hank Trotter and how he'd helped Geoff develop his skills. Stephanie liked that he was so willing to give credit where it was due.

"I don't know if you've noticed," the host said, "but there's a lot of interest in your personal life." He smiled mischievously as if he'd been biding his time until he could turn to this salacious gossip and Stephanie held her breath as she anticipated the rest of the inquiry. "You've been spotted kissing a young woman at the rodeo. From what we hear, she was your nurse after your shoulder surgery. What can you tell us about your relationship?"

For someone who'd known he was going to be interviewed, Geoff seemed stumped by the question. Surely he had to have known he would be asked about their relationship. The picture of them kissing had gone viral, along with the accompanying article linking them together. Curiosity about her had been the reason that a reporter had dug around in her past until she'd found an ex-boyfriend willing to trash her reputation. And then there was his former flame's interview. Given that, now was the time for Geoff to tell the world how much he cared about Stephanie and get rid of that question once and for all.

"I prefer to keep my private life private."

"I'm not asking for intimate details," the host pressed on. "I just want to know if there is a relationship or not."

"Come on, man."

"I'm not asking for me. I'm asking for all the single women out there who want to know if they have a chance with you. So are you serious about this woman or not?"

Geoff gave a little laugh and shook his head. "Next question, please."

The host grinned ruefully. "Well, you can't blame me for trying."

As the interview turned to the rodeo and its increasing diversity. Stephanie heard nothing. Her mind whirled in confusion. Her emotions bounced from relief to anger to disappointment without settling on one for more than a few seconds. And while her feelings changed with each breath, several questions rattled around in her brain. Why had Geoff refused to talk about her? It almost seemed as if he was denying their relationship.

Was he trying to protect her privacy? If so, it was much too late. That ship had sailed long ago. Or was he simply making it known that he wasn't committed to her? After all, hadn't his ex-girlfriend stated that Geoff couldn't be trusted in the long run? And Geoff hadn't denied it. He'd simply avoided the conversation altogether.

Perhaps he didn't want the entire world to know that they were serious about each other. Were they serious? Or had she created an entire relationship in her mind? It was possible. She'd witnessed other women manufacture a relationship out of thin air. They'd mistaken sex for love, a short affair for a budding relationship. Before long, they had convinced themselves that they were a proposal short of living happily ever after. In reality, the man had simply been having fun, enjoying dating an interesting woman before moving on.

Was that happening here? Had she convinced herself that she and Geoff were on the verge of a serious relationship when none was on the horizon? After all, he'd said that he wasn't interested in anything permanent. Her mind spun in such circles, her head began to hurt. She closed her eyes and forced the negative thoughts away, but by the time she started watching again, the interview was over and Geoff was reminding the audience to check out the rodeo when it came to town.

Her stomach churned and her heart ached as the negative thoughts returned with a vengeance. She wanted to believe in Geoff, but after what she'd seen and heard, her doubts and fears were magnified. She wanted to believe what he felt for her was different from what he'd felt for Cynthia and the other women who'd come before her, but nothing in his response gave her hope. And that was crushing.

She turned off the television and went to her room. She was just settling into her bed for what she knew would be a night of tossing and turning when her phone rang. She checked the caller ID before answering.

"I hope it's not too late to call."

Although it was good to hear Geoff's voice, her doubts remained. "No. I'm still awake."

"Did you see the interview?"

"Yes." Although now, she wished that she hadn't. Geoff's *next question, please* had made an indelible mark on her heart, feeding the doubts about their relationship. Those words would echo in her brain for days if not weeks to come. She'd worried that a celebrity wouldn't be serious about a small-town regular girl. Maybe she shouldn't have ignored those fears. If she'd been smarter then, her heart wouldn't be aching now.

He paused as if waiting for her to say more. What could he possibly expect her to say? Did he want her to tell him that she'd fallen in love with him? That her heart was breaking because he was making it clear that he didn't feel the same? When the silence dragged on, she thought about asking where she stood, but she quickly dismissed the notion. She had her pride. "You did a good job informing people about the diversity in rodeo," she settled for saying. Neutral was better.

"Then it was all worth it."

What was all worth it? Putting up with questions about her?

Her doubts were getting the best of her so she feigned a yawn.

"You're tired. I'll let you get some sleep. I'll see you tomorrow."

"Good night." Stephanie hung up the phone. Despite her doubts, she felt a flare of hope when he mentioned seeing her tomorrow. Even so, the nagging sensation didn't totally vanish. Geoff was saying all the right things to her. So why did she still think there might be something to what his ex-girlfriend had said?

Stephanie parked her car in front of her parents' house and then grabbed the peach cobbler that she'd made for the Brandt Thanksgiving Day dinner. Although she didn't have as much time to cook as she would have liked, she enjoyed baking and often took dessert to work to share with her coworkers. Everyone knew to expect a cheesecake on their birthday.

She didn't bother with the doorbell; rather she turned the knob and stepped inside. She'd hoped to find her mother alone so that she could talk to her, but she should have known better. Her brothers were already present and accounted for, sprawled in the best seats in the house as they watched the football pregame show. If she lived to be a hundred, she would never understand how or why guys could sit around and watch people talk about a game that hadn't even happened yet. What could they possibly say for three hours? But then she still couldn't fathom how a sixty-minute game took three times that long.

"Hey," Ethan said, standing to give her a kiss on the cheek while simultaneously reaching for the peach cobbler. "Let me help you with that."

She laughed and held the dish out of her brother's grasp. "I'm not falling for that. If I let you take it, the rest of the family won't get a bite."

He placed a hand over his heart and sighed dramatically. "I'm hurt and offended that you would question my chivalry."

"And yet you haven't denied it."

Grinning, Ethan sat back down while Stephanie put the dessert on the coffee table and took off her coat.

"Where's the cowboy?" Lucas asked.

Questions about Geoff already? She'd barely gotten in the door.

"He's still in LA. His plane should take off soon. Why?"

"I saw him on television last night. He was pretty slick with his answers. A little too slick." Her brothers had seemed to like Geoff when they'd met him. But Lucas's cold eyes didn't hold any affection at the moment.

"What's that supposed to mean?"

"It means that I saw his ex on TV the other

night. She accused him of leading her on. It also means that I'll break his other arm if he's messing with my sister."

"Don't be a caveman."

"Call me what you want, but I mean what I say."

"Did you happen to read the tabloid article where I was accused of being a gold digger?"

Lucas waved his hand. "Yeah, I read that nonsense. If Aaron has any sense, he'll change his name and move across the country. Because if I catch him—"

"While I appreciate your sudden and totally out-of-character need to spill blood, you're missing my point. None of what was written about me was true. But that didn't stop that rag from printing it. The same can be true of Geoff. We don't know what happened between them." And not for want of her asking, but she wouldn't tell Lucas that. Especially since his words made it harder to dismiss her doubts.

Lucas shrugged. He didn't look convinced. "Could be. But he's not my sister. You are. Which means my loyalty is to you."

Stephanie sighed, grabbed her cobbler, and then went into the kitchen where her parents were. Thank goodness they'd always been reasonable people, not controlled by emotions. They would help her put her feelings in perspective. Otherwise this would be the longest Thanksgiving of her life.

"What do you have there?" her father asked from his seat at the table, pausing briefly from peeling sweet potatoes.

When Stephanie and her siblings were growing up, her parents had put in long hours at work. Now that they were older and more successful, Phillip and Mallory Brandt spent less time at the office and more time at home. Her father had even begun cooking dinner, and he was surprisingly good.

"Peach cobbler."

"Put it in the refrigerator if you can find space," her mother said, turning from the stove where she was stirring seasonings into a pot of ham hocks and greens. Steam and the aroma of smoked meat filled the air.

Stephanie pulled open the refrigerator and after shifting a couple of dishes around, she was able to get her pan inside. "I didn't expect Lucas and Ethan to be here so early."

"I don't know why not. It's the same way every year."

"True." But Stephanie hadn't been here last Thanksgiving because she'd had to work.

Stephanie heard the dogs barking in the yard and looked outside. Her parents' black labs were running around with Lucas's mastiff. "I can't believe Lucas brought that enormous dog of his."

"You know Flash is his baby."

Stephanie washed her hands and then grabbed

a knife from a drawer and began to peel apples for pies.

"So where's Geoff?" her mother asked, brushing a tendril of hair away from her face. "You invited him to dinner, didn't you?"

"I did. He's still in LA. He promised to be back in time."

Her parents exchanged a look and her father's lips turned down slightly. What was that about? Her parents hadn't even met Geoff. They were normally such welcoming people. But Stephanie thought about Lucas's attitude and dread gnawed at her stomach. Perhaps her parents hadn't been overly impressed by the interview, either. Maybe she was right to have doubts.

"Okay," her father said finally.

"What's going on?"

Her parents passed a surreptitious look between them. "We saw him on television," her mother said. "He seemed pretty evasive when it came to talking about you."

The marble-size ball of nerves in her stomach grew to the size of a baseball. Still she wasn't ready to admit that she agreed with her parents. "I wouldn't say that. We just agreed to keep our relationship private. You know I don't like people knowing all my business. And I distinctly remember you both telling us all of our lives to guard our privacy."

She'd absorbed that lesson along with the others her parents had drilled into her and her siblings. Along with not sharing her personal business far and wide, they'd also taught her the importance of a good name. Which was one of the reasons she'd been so upset that the tabloid had published lies about her. To her enormous relief, her parents hadn't been upset about the article. But they were clearly upset now.

"There's a big difference between maintaining your privacy and denying a relationship altogether," her mother added.

Stephanie was confused. Her parents had always been so open-minded. They'd accepted each person she and her siblings had dated over the years. They hadn't blinked an eye when Brittany brought home Daniel Dubois, along with Hailey, his sweet baby niece, and announced that they were engaged to be married in a few weeks' time. What had happened to those parents? She needed them to convince her that her doubts were unfounded. She needed their assurance that she wasn't going to end up with a broken heart.

She shook her head. Her nerves were approaching soccer ball size, but she infused her words with as much confidence as she could. "I don't think he did that."

"Not in so many words," her father said.

"Really, Dad? You sound just like Lucas."

Her mom blew out a breath. "You're right. We're being overprotective."

"I know," Stephanie said, hoping there was no reason for them to be. "And when Geoff gets here please be nice to him."

"Have we ever been anything else?" her father asked.

"No. But everyone can have an off day."

Her dad nodded toward the living room. "Sounds like you've been watching football with your brothers."

"Please. One sport at a time is all I can handle." And apparently that sport was now rodeo.

Her parents exchanged glances again—silently communicating with each other—and Stephanie wondered if that simple comment revealed more than she'd intended it to. Before she could give that any thought, there was a commotion as Hailey burst into the kitchen. "Paw Paw, cookie."

Phillip Brandt wiped his hands on a towel and then raced to pick up Hailey. "How's Grandpa's baby girl?"

Hailey grinned and then placed a sloppy kiss on his cheek before turning to her grandmother. "Nana. Cookie?"

"How about a hug first?"

Hailey lunged for the older woman. Stephanie marveled as her parents expertly transferred the toddler from one grandparent to the other. "What kind of cookie do you want?"

"Big."

"Okay."

Brittany and Daniel stepped into the kitchen and Stephanie shared an exasperated grin with her sister. "What happened to the parents who raised us? You know, the ones who thought that raisins were snacks and cookies were desserts?"

"They became grandparents," Brittany said.

"That's right," their mother said, taking a homemade chocolate chip cookie from a plate and handing it to Hailey. Once she'd settled the little girl in her high chair, she filled a sippy cup with milk and set it on the tray. "Rules are for children, not grandchildren. Grandchildren are for spoiling."

"On that note, what can I do to help?" Brittany asked.

"Finish setting the table. We'll be ready to eat at about three." Mallory looked back at Stephanie. "Will Geoff be here by then?"

"He should. His plane should be in the air by now."

Her mother nodded and Stephanie followed Brittany into the dining room and helped her set the table.

"So what's wrong?" Brittany asked as they folded cloth napkins and set them on the china. Their mother had a set of dishes for each holiday.

The ones devoted to Thanksgiving had always been Stephanie's favorite.

"Everyone's hassling me about Geoff." Stephanie raised a hand, preempting her sister before she could say anything negative. "If you're going to join the chorus, please don't."

"I had no intention of doing that. Why would I?"

"The interview last night."

Brittany nodded. "We watched it. He looks good on television."

"That's all you have to say? You aren't going to go on about how evasive he was about me and our relationship?" Stephanie mentally crossed her fingers. She needed someone to be positive about the relationship and tell her that she could trust Geoff.

"Look at who I married. Daniel does his very best to avoid the spotlight. And he's even more diligent when it comes to protecting me and Hailey from the press. Geoff clearly was doing the same thing."

"You're the only one who thinks that."

"No, she's not."

Stephanie turned at her younger sister's voice. She'd been so involved in the conversation that she hadn't heard Tiffany enter the room. "Hey. How long have you been here?"

"Long enough to eavesdrop on your conversation. I agree with Brittany. Geoff was protecting your privacy."

Stephanie appreciated her sisters' support, but it only went so far in ending her discomfort. Brittany was a happy newlywed and Tiffany had always been a hopeless romantic, so they saw the world through rose-colored glasses. Neither of them could be completely objective. And though she didn't want to admit it, her parents and Lucas had only been giving voice to her concern. The doubts that had appeared last night after watching the interview were still as strong today. She'd hoped her parents would tell her that she was being foolish. They hadn't done that, which only increased her doubts.

The sisters changed the subject as they finished setting the table, then put a cloth on the buffet in preparation for the serving dishes that wouldn't fit on the table. There was a running joke in the family that on holidays her mother made everything that she knew how to cook. Even though they made fun, everyone was more than happy to take home enough leftovers to last for two days.

They went into the living room and joined her brothers. Every once in a while, Stephanie sneaked a look at her phone, hoping to find a text from Geoff. Nothing. She hadn't expected him to call as soon as he landed, but how much effort would it take to shoot off a text? On a certain level she knew she was being foolish, but she'd just defended him to her parents and Lucas. Right now she was worried it might come back and bite her on the butt.

Her mom came into the living room. "Help get the food on the table so we can eat."

Ethan, Lucas and Daniel jumped to their feet. Stephanie glanced at the front door, willing the doorbell to ring. When she realized that her brothers and brother-in-law were watching her with something akin to pity, she lowered her eyes and picked an imaginary piece of lint off her sweater before following them into the kitchen. They were putting the last platters onto the buffet when the doorbell rang.

"I'll get it," Stephanie said, rushing from the room. When she reached the door, she glanced into the mirror in the entry even though it was too late to do anything to fix her appearance. Luckily her makeup and hair were still perfect. She was wearing a purple sweater, black leggings and black boots. Her large silver hoop earrings matched her silver chain necklace. Satisfied that she looked good, she opened the door and smiled.

"Hey," Geoff said, leaning over and brushing a soft kiss against her lips. "I hope I'm not too late."

"You're right on time. We were just sitting down to eat."

"The plane sat on the tarmac for nearly a half an hour. But we'd pushed away from the gate so technically we departed on time." That explained that.

Geoff was holding two bouquets of flowers.

"These are for you," he said, handing her a dozen red roses. "And these are for your mother."

Stephanie smiled. Her mother loved flowers. Hopefully this colorful bouquet would help Mallory warm up to Geoff. Taking his free hand, Stephanie led him into the dining room and introduced him to the members of her family that he hadn't yet met. Her mother exclaimed delightedly over the flowers and quickly put them in a vase while dishes were shifted to make a place for them at the center of the table.

Once grace was said, there was commotion as food was passed around the table and plates filled. The conversation was stilted at first and Stephanie's heart practically stopped beating. Then Daniel mentioned the interview and asked Geoff how he could stand being so famous.

Geoff looked at everyone before answering. "It's part of the job. I like being a part of rodeo and count it a privilege to make a wider audience aware of the contributions of Black riders. If it means I have to step out of my comfort zone and be uncomfortable for a while in order to educate the public, I'll do it."

That answer seemed to meet with her family's approval and after that the conversation flowed more easily. Even so, Stephanie knew her parents well enough to know that they still had their doubts about Geoff. They'd always been good judges of character, so that didn't help with *her* doubts. Even though her family had been polite to Geoff, Stephanie was unable to completely relax. By the time they'd finished dinner she was emotionally drained.

Shortly after dinner was over, Stephanie's mother pressed a plate of leftovers into her hands. Stephanie kissed her father's cheek and then said goodbye to her siblings. She and Geoff walked side by side to her car.

"Do you want to follow me to my parents' house?" he asked as he opened her door.

Stephanie inhaled deeply and then blew out a breath. The tension from the past few hours had caught up with her and all she wanted to do was soak in a warm tub until her skin was wrinkled and then watch old sci-fi movies on television until she'd thoroughly decompressed. "Actually," she began, fighting against the guilt she felt when he stiffened, "I need a rain check. I'm really worn out and I don't think I'd be good company. I just want to go home. Would you please make my apologies to your parents?"

Geoff heard the words coming from Stephanie's mouth, but he couldn't believe what she was saying. Was she really going to bail on him? He stared at her. Though she claimed to be tired, she looked like her usual sparkling self. She'd been radiant at dinner and he'd been mesmerized by her beauty. More than once, he'd had to remind himself to lift his fork to his mouth and eat instead of just staring at her. He hoped Mallory hadn't noticed. The last thing he wanted was to have her believe that he hadn't liked her food. It had been delicious, second only to his mother's.

But as happy as he was to be with Stephanie, he sensed that she didn't feel the same. She seemed to be on edge. He knew things had been a bit tense between them before he'd left—thanks to Cynthia's lies—but he'd believed they'd been putting that behind them. Before Cynthia's interview, Stephanie had enjoyed being with him. Now she was pushing him away. Was she trying to back out of the relationship? He didn't know, but now wasn't the time to ask her. They needed privacy, which they didn't have now. They were standing in the middle of the street in front of her parents' house and he could see at least one member of her family standing in the window watching them.

"Okay. I'll call you later." He considered kissing her, but changed his mind. He wasn't altogether sure she wouldn't turn her head away, which would be more disappointment than he could endure for the night.

As Geoff drove to his parents' house, he kept replaying the events of the afternoon, wondering how they could have had a different outcome. He wouldn't be in Bronco for much longer and time spent with Stephanie was precious to him. Yet she was acting as if he didn't mean a thing to her.

He parked the car and then sat there a moment as he tried to gain control of his emotions. His mother was happy to have all of her sons home for Thanksgiving and he didn't want to bring her down. He took several deep breaths before getting out of the car.

They'd already finished eating dinner and his brothers and father were in the living room watching the football game. Apparently something happened in the game because Ross and Jack cheered while Mike and their father shook their heads in disgust.

Geoff said hello, then went into the kitchen where his mother was sitting at the table, sipping a cup of coffee and doing a crossword puzzle. She looked up and smiled. "Where's Stephanie?"

He shook his head and slumped into a chair. "She was a little tired, so she asked me to apologize for her absence."

"She does work long hours."

"Yeah."

Jeanne leaned back and then gave him a knowing look. "So why do you look like you've lost your best friend?"

Geoff blew out a deep breath. She knew him so well. "Because although that sounds like a plausible explanation, I think there's more to it than that."

"What do you think is going on?"

"I don't know. She seemed stressed at dinner with her family."

"In what way?"

He shrugged as he sat down at the table. "I don't know. It almost seemed as if she was waiting for something to go wrong."

"And did it?"

"No. Her sisters and brother-in-law were very friendly and her parents and brothers were very... polite."

"Why the pause?"

"I've met her brothers before. They were much friendlier. But at dinner, they seemed cool."

"Maybe they saw the interview."

"Stephanie told me they did."

"That might account for some of the difference you sensed."

"I can't believe they would put so much stock in Cynthia's lies."

"That was a mess, but that's not the interview I was talking about."

"Then which one?"

"Yours. Last night."

"Why? That doesn't make sense. I was very careful to protect Stephanie's privacy, which I know really matters to her."

Jeanne chuckled. "That may be what you intended, but that's not the way it came across."

Geoff thought back to the interview. He hadn't said anything about Stephanie, despite the host's many attempts to pry information from him.

Ross walked into the kitchen and opened the refrigerator, taking out a sweet potato pie.

"Is it halftime yet?" Jeanne asked.

"It's just starting. And not a moment too soon. I need a break from listening to Dad and Mike complain about the officials."

"Good. I want Geoff to see his interview from last night."

"I don't want to watch that," Geoff balked. "You know I hate seeing myself on television."

"Why? You look so adorable," Ross teased.

"You need to see this," Jeanne insisted. "Then maybe it will become clear what I mean."

Shaking his head, Geoff followed his mother into the living room. There was some general groaning when his mother turned away from the halftime show. "You don't need to hear people talk about the game you just saw. And why are you guys in the living room instead of the man cave?"

Nobody had an answer for that, so they stopped complaining.

Jeanne turned on the DVR and sped to the part of the program where Geoff was introduced and then paused the replay. Geoff never watched himself on TV and always turned the channel when one of his commercials came on.

His mother patted the couch beside her. "Have a seat."

When he was sitting, she hit Play. He couldn't imagine what he would see that would alter the way he remembered it, but he was desperate to understand what Stephanie was thinking. Besides, his mother was seldom wrong about matters of the heart. If she said watching his interview was necessary to understand what went wrong, then it was necessary.

He watched attentively, looking for clues that he might be giving off, remembering how he felt during the talk.

The host asked about Stephanie, and Geoff said he wanted to keep his relationship private. The host had asked a couple of questions about his injury and then steered the conversation back to Stephanie, asking if he was serious about her. Geoff watched the screen as he shook his head and gave a little laugh.

Oh, no. No wonder they'd acted as they had. Appalled, he looked at his mother. His head began to throb. If blood could actually run cold, his would be frozen in his veins. He'd ruined everything. "That's not... I didn't mean I wasn't serious about Stephanie."

"You laughed and shook your head as if that

was a ridiculous question. And given the things that Cynthia said about you, it's easy for Stephanie to think that she doesn't mean much to you. And if I were her mother, I wouldn't be very warm to you, either."

"I didn't know it came across like that. I couldn't believe he wouldn't let the matter drop. When he asked if it was serious, the word seemed so inadequate that I couldn't help but shake my head and smile."

"So are you serious about Stephanie?"

"Yes." He didn't need to think about it. He didn't know how or when it happened, but he'd fallen in love with Stephanie. She meant the world to him and he would do anything to make her happy. Instead, he'd hurt her horribly and made her doubt his feelings for her. And because of how he'd come across in this stupid interview, she'd never believe his feelings were real.

"Well, you need to do something to convince her. Because no matter what you were thinking, it looked for all the world like you were saying she wasn't important to you."

"How do I fix that?"

Jeanne smiled. "I can't tell you that. That's something you have to figure out on your own. But next time make sure that you say what you mean."

"That's a given." He kissed his mother's cheek

and stood. Now that he knew what the problem was, he could fix it.

He just had to come up with a plan. Because one way or another, he was going to win back his girl.

Chapter Thirteen

Geoff called Stephanie that night, but she must have been asleep because she didn't answer. At least that was what he hoped. He hated to think that he'd messed up so badly that she was avoiding him. That thought kept him awake most of the night. The next morning he considered going to see her at the hospital, but decided against it. She didn't need her personal life bleeding into her professional one. Besides, even if they could talk, it wouldn't be for more than a few minutes. He needed more than her break time to explain. As much as he hated the idea, he would have to wait until this evening to clear the air.

Unable to think of anything else, he spent the morning developing a strategy for convincing Stephanie that he truly cared for her. He'd just about come up with the right plan when his agent called with what he referred to as "great news." He'd just finalized a sponsorship deal with a major athletic clothing brand. They'd been working out the details for a while and Geoff was thrilled. That was until Troy explained that Geoff needed to meet with the sponsor in New York that evening. His agent had already arranged a flight for that afternoon.

Geoff frowned. "Is there a way to move the meeting?"

"Are you kidding me? We've been trying to close this deal forever and a day. They want to meet with you and shake hands on it tonight."

Geoff blew out a breath. There went the plans he had to spend the evening with Stephanie.

"Okay. I'll be there."

He hung up the phone and then went to his bedroom where he began throwing clothes into a suitcase. He looked up to see his father standing there.

"Going somewhere?"

"Yes." As Geoff grabbed his boots, he explained about the meeting that evening.

"When will you be back?"

"I don't know. I start back on the tour Monday." Although he wasn't going to be competing, he would be fulfilling promotional obligations. "I was hoping to have a couple more days here."

"I know. Your brothers are leaving in the morning." His father patted him on the shoulder. "It was good to have you boys home again."

"It was good to be here. I'll be back as soon as I can. In fact, if things work out, I'll be spending a lot more time here in Bronco."

"Your mother will be glad to hear that."

"Just Mom?"

His dad grinned. "Well, you know, I like having my wife all to myself."

Geoff laughed at him. "I guess I'd better tell her I'm leaving."

After saying his goodbyes, Geoff got Mike to take him to the airport. As he was unfastening his seat belt, Mike grabbed him by the arm. When Geoff looked at him, his brother's expression was serious. "Straighten things out with Stephanie before it's too late. She's a good woman and we all like her. You don't want her to get away."

Geoff nodded and got out of the car. "I'm going to do my best."

The plane was loading when Geoff reached the gate, so he didn't get a chance to call Stephanie. He hated that, but it couldn't be helped. Besides, he intended to talk to her before the night was over.

Stephanie checked her phone one more time, hoping against hope that there would be a missed call or text from Geoff. Nothing. Telling herself that the sound she heard wasn't her heart breaking, she put on her coat and slammed her locker door shut. Luckily she'd had to spend a few more minutes with a patient and everyone from her shift had already left. She'd kept up a brave front all day, but she didn't know how much longer she would be able to pretend that everything was okay when she felt miserable.

Though she was trying to keep the faith and believe that he had feelings for her, it was harder to do given mounting evidence to the contrary. Her head was telling her to open her eyes and see what was right in front of her—what Cynthia had described with her relationship with Geoff was happening to Stephanie—but her heart wasn't that smart. She didn't want to believe that Geoff had been lying to her about his feelings. Perhaps she was a fool to still care about him, but she did.

When she got home, she changed into a pair of sweats, heated up leftovers and dropped onto the couch. She turned on the television and quickly searched for something to distract her from the questions cycling through her brain. She settled on a marathon of reruns of one of her favorite sci-fi shows. She'd seen every episode at least a hundred times and wouldn't have to try hard to follow the plot. More importantly, there was nothing remotely romantic going to happen, so she knew there wouldn't be any reminders of her flailing relationship.

When she caught herself checking her phone for texts, she turned it off. If Geoff had intended to contact her, he would have done so by now. The fact that he hadn't spoke volumes.

She watched several episodes, not quite distracting herself. When she found herself nodding

off, she got into bed where she tossed and turned
all night.

The next morning she wasn't the least bit re-
freshed, but since it was her day off, she didn't
sweat it. She made fast work of cleaning her house
and was debating whether to brave the crowds to
get deals on Christmas gifts when her doorbell
rang. *Geoff.* Her heart was thudding in her chest
and she raced to the door and swung it open. She
tried to swallow her disappointment when she
spotted a delivery man on the way back to his
truck. She looked down and spotted a package.

Grabbing it, she closed the door behind her and
went inside. The return label was that of Beaumont
and Rossi's Fine Jewels in downtown Bronco. Although she'd occasionally saved and splurged on
items on sale there, she hadn't purchased anything
recently. She checked to be sure that the package
hadn't been left at the wrong door, but it was ad-
dressed to her.

She ripped open the brown paper and revealed
a gaily wrapped box. Curiouser and curiouser.
There was a small envelope with her name on it.
Despite the fact that she was eager to know what
was inside the box she was more eager to know
who sent it. She slipped her fingernail under the
closure and pulled out a card. *Thinking of you.
Missing you. Geoff.*

Geoff had sent her a present. Her heart began

to sing even as her doubts surged. Hadn't Cynthia said that Geoff had given her gifts? That was part of his modus operandi. Had they moved to the next stage of his obviously well-rehearsed stage play?

Despite the battle raging between her head and her heart, with her head telling her not to be misled and her heart telling her to trust, she opened the box. A sterling silver charm bracelet was nestled on a layer of cotton. She reached inside and held the jewelry in her hands. There were two charms. One was a Christmas tree and the other was a star. The charms reminded her of the day they'd spent at the ranch where he'd learned to ride. The day she'd begun to believe she was special to him. Unable to resist, she put on the bracelet and then held out her arm.

Telling herself she was only calling him because it would be rude not to thank him for the gift and not because she was a fool and desperate to hear his voice, she grabbed her phone. She hadn't turned it back on.

There were three messages from him. The first had been left fifteen minutes after she'd turned off the phone last night. He'd had to leave town for business and wanted to let her know that he'd been thinking of her. He'd hoped they could talk. He'd called her twice more last night.

Even her sensible head agreed that there was

no reason not to call him now since he'd called her first. As his phone rang, she tried to figure out what it was that he'd wanted to tell her last night.

"Stephanie." The sound of his voice sent tingles skipping down her spine. They might have a lot of things to work out, but one thing hadn't changed—her body still wanted him. And it was just as stubborn as her heart.

"Hi. I got your gift."

"Do you like it?"

"I do."

He paused. "I'm sorry that I had to leave town so suddenly. My agent has been working on this sponsorship opportunity for months and everything came together yesterday. I'm actually in New York now."

"Wow."

"I hated to leave town without seeing you, but it couldn't be helped. Everything happened at the last minute."

"I understand." She managed to keep her voice neutral.

"When I leave here, I won't be back in Bronco for a week. I'll see you when I get back. Okay?"

"Sure." It was happening already. Geoff was getting his life back on track. A life that was spent traveling across the country. He was looking forward. Soon she would only be visible to him in his rearview mirror.

There was a pause before Geoff spoke again, his voice distracted. "I need to get going."

When the call ended, Stephanie stared at the bracelet. Was giving her this piece of jewelry his way of letting her down easy? It would definitely fit the pattern Cynthia described. Her heart broke at the thought. Without warning, she burst into tears. This wasn't the ending she'd envisioned when she'd gotten involved with Geoff. Perhaps it should have been. Then she wouldn't have let herself fall in love with him.

The next day, Geoff sent her a carved music box that played "Jingle Bells." She wound it and listened to it repeatedly as if trying to convince herself that her hope—and love—weren't misplaced. On December 1, he sent her an advent calendar. Since it was the first day of advent, she opened the box for that day. Inside was a lovely pair of earrings, shaped like reindeer. Silencing her ever-present doubt, she put them in her ears. The following day she opened the next box to discover a locket in the shape of a sleigh. Another gift arrived, as well—a crystal nativity scene which she put in a place of honor on the coffee table in her living room.

Although she loved her daily presents, it was hearing from Geoff that brightened her days and worked on silencing her doubts although they never went away. The last time they'd spoken, he'd told her that he expected to be home soon. She hoped so. Though he was acting like he cared about her, she couldn't get his interview out of her mind. He'd never explained why he'd shaken his head and laughed. She wanted to believe the gifts were proof that she mattered to him, but she kept hearing his former girlfriend's words echoing in her mind. Geoff had showered Cynthia with presents too, and then he'd dumped her unexpectedly. At least that was what Cynthia had said. Geoff had denied it. But still…was this part of a pattern?

Thankfully her doorbell rang, stopping her before she could begin traveling down that negative path. She pulled the door open and gasped. Geoff was standing on her porch, a dozen red roses in his arms. He looked so good that she couldn't move. Couldn't talk. Couldn't breathe.

"Hi. Are you going to let me in?"

"Of course." She shook off her stupor and let him in. "I didn't expect you back today."

"I wanted to surprise you." He removed his coat and then kissed her gently.

Although she wanted to throw herself into his arms and lean into the kiss, she held back. She needed to know where she stood. "Let's sit down."

"Don't you want to put the flowers in a vase?"

What she wanted was to get to the heart of the matter, but she supposed it would be better to ease into the conversation.

He followed her into the kitchen while she put the flowers in water, watching but not speaking. When that was done, they returned to the living room and sat down. She hated the awkwardness between them, but until he'd made his feelings clear—whatever they were—she wouldn't be able to regain her previous ease. "I missed you," he said.

"Did you?" She wished she could take him at his word, but she couldn't. She still had too many questions.

"Yes. Did you doubt that?"

She shrugged. "We barely know each other. I've only been a part of your life for a few weeks."

"And you think that makes you forgettable?"

"I think it makes it easier for you to get back to your regular life that doesn't include me."

He shook his head and laughed. Just like he'd done in the interview, and her doubts returned in full force.

"I guess this is funny to you," she said, starting to get to her feet.

He grabbed her arm. "Not at all."

"You laughed. Again. Just like you did on national television."

"Yeah. I wasn't laughing because it was funny."

She raised an eyebrow at his non-explanation.

"And about that interview," he continued. "I wasn't denying my feelings for you. I was trying to protect your privacy. I know you don't want the details of our relationship splashed across tabloids. Our feelings are private."

That was true. "You never told me how you felt."

He turned her face to his. "I thought the gifts would show you know how I felt."

"Gifts are nice, but I told you that I don't need things." Besides, he'd showered Cynthia with gifts and that relationship hadn't lasted.

"I believed you, but I guess I didn't *really* believe you. You're the first woman who I've actually wanted to give gifts to and they don't matter that much to you."

"They matter. And I appreciate them. But…"

"But what?"

"I don't know." She didn't feel comfortable enough to put her feelings into words. She had fallen in love with him, but she didn't know how he felt. She wasn't willing to go out on a limb just yet.

"Did you like the advent calendar?"

"Yes. I liked everything." Did he not understand what she had been saying to him? Could he not see how much he had come to matter to her? The presents were nice, but she was talking about her feelings here. The fact that he was focused more on things than emotions gave her pause. Her feelings were obviously stronger than his.

"Did you open all of the boxes?"

"Of course not. That's not how advent calendars work. You're only supposed to open one box a day." She tried to cover her disappointment, but she couldn't. Maybe this was hopeless. She and Geoff were too different for a relationship between them to work.

Geoff looked at Stephanie. When she'd opened the door, her face had been alight with happiness. Her smile had been bright and her eyes had glowed. She'd been overjoyed to see him. Now her face was unreadable. She'd shut down emotionally. He didn't know what he had done wrong, but he knew he'd somehow managed to kill the mood. The last thing he wanted was more misunderstanding and confusion between them. She meant too much to him to let a simple misunderstanding trash their relationship.

He recalled his mother's advice. She'd told him to say what he meant. He hadn't. Instead, he'd turned to gifts, hoping Stephanie would recognize the emotions behind them. He'd been wrong. He now knew that sincerely spoken words meant more than any gift he could ever give her.

He just hoped it wasn't too late to salvage their relationship.

"I'm sorry," he said.

"For what?"

"For not being clear about my feelings. I should have told you how I felt before now."

She smiled tentatively and he could tell that although she was warming up to him, she still had reservations. How had he done such a poor job of conveying his feelings to her? He knew that Cynthia's lies had been a major part of it, but his interview hadn't helped. His attempt to protect her privacy had backfired spectacularly. He'd planned to wait but...

The advent calendar was on the table beside the sofa. "I was going to wait until Christmas, but I can't. Now seems like the time."

"Time to what?" Clearly he'd confused her with his abrupt change of topic.

He picked up the calendar and handed it to her. "Open the box for Christmas Day."

"What? No. That's cheating."

"Just do it."

Sighing and muttering to herself that it was wrong to open the boxes out of order and not at all how advent calendars worked, Stephanie opened the box. Geoff's heart was in his throat as he waited for her to look inside.

Stephanie lifted the top, looked inside and gasped. Then she looked up at him, a question in her lovely eyes.

He took the box from her and pulled out a princess-cut diamond ring in a platinum setting. "I know we haven't known each other long, but it's been long enough to be certain of how I feel. I love you, Stephanie. You're the first person I think about each day, and the last person I think about each night. You live in my heart. You *own* my heart. If you'll marry me, I'll spend every waking moment trying to make you happy." He inhaled and then continued. "I know it might be hard at first since my career requires me to travel a lot, but my commitment to you is unwavering. My feelings won't change." He paused and shook his head. "No, that's not right. They will change. They'll grow stronger for you every day."

Geoff looked at Stephanie and was surprised to see her eyes fill with tears. His heart sank as he tried to figure out what he'd said wrong. Or had he read the situation wrong? Maybe she wasn't in love with him.

And then she smiled, and his heart lifted. "Yes. Oh, yes."

Geoff knelt and took her left hand and then gently slid the ring onto her slender finger. It fit perfectly. Then he lifted her hand to his lips and kissed it. The blood surged through his veins and he pulled her down to kiss her lips. She moaned against his mouth and his desire grew. He slid his arms beneath her knees and in one smooth motion, he sat and pulled her onto his lap, deepening the kiss. All of the confusion and misunderstanding between them disappeared in that moment.

Then suddenly he felt her pulling away and

he reluctantly released her. She eased off his lap, stood and offered her hand. He looked into her beautiful face and she smiled at him. "I think we'll be more comfortable in my bed. Don't you agree?"

He jumped to his feet. She didn't have to tell him twice. Besides, there were some things that words alone couldn't say. "Definitely."

They walked side by side to her room where he told her and showed her just how much he loved her.

Later as she was lying his arms, he turned to her. "We should go somewhere to celebrate."

"I like the way we just celebrated."

He laughed. "True. That was great."

"Where do you want to go?"

"I don't know about you, but I'm seriously hungry."

She laughed ruefully. "I have to admit that my appetite has been missing the past few days."

He ran a finger across her bare shoulder. "Because you missed me?"

"If I say yes, will that inflate your ego?"

"No. It'll make me feel better because I'll know I wasn't alone in missing you."

"Then yes, I missed you. I missed you so much I couldn't breathe. I wanted to believe that you cared about me, but it was hard."

He kissed her and then pulled her into his arms. When he thought about how he'd hurt her, his heart ached. Especially when he'd only been trying to protect her. Knowing that it was possible to cause her pain without meaning to made him determined to be better in the future than he'd been in the past.

"But you know I love you, right?" he asked. He had never said those words to another woman. Now he couldn't say them enough.

"Yes."

He lifted her hand. "And if you ever start to doubt that again, let me know and I'll remind you."

"I will."

They smiled at each other before she tossed the blankets aside and grabbed her robe. "Now let's get some food."

After a quick shower and an even quicker discussion while they dressed, they decided to go to Doug's to celebrate their engagement. After all, that had been the part of their first date that had convinced Stephanie that he was the type of guy she wanted in her life.

Doug's was decked out for Christmas, giving the run-down building a festive appearance. The interior was decorated, too. Lights and garland were draped on the walls and along the front of the bar. The scarred tables had been covered with green plastic tablecloths with an artificial poinsettia set in the middle. Even the haunted bar stool had garland wrapped around it. It was still behind caution tape, though. They glanced at the stool at the same time and Stephanie smiled. "Maybe you broke the curse when you sat on it."

"Maybe. But I don't think you'll convince Doug of that."

"Hey," the crowd called out as Geoff and Stephanie stepped inside.

Geoff and Stephanie greeted their friends then sat down at an empty table. When their waitress came, they ordered buffalo wings and pizza.

"So, what brings you here?" Doug called from the bar.

Geoff wanted to share the great news with everyone he knew, but he paused. Stephanie was a private person. Although most of the other patrons were Geoff's friends, there were also people he didn't know. Would Stephanie want them to know her business? Before he answered Doug's question, he glanced at Stephanie. She smiled and shrugged. "Go ahead."

"You don't mind if they know before we tell our families?"

"We can do that next. Good news doesn't run out. Our families will be just as happy for us even if they aren't first to know."

He leaned across the table and kissed her lips. "I don't know how I got so lucky."

"You must be living right."

Geoff turned and looked at Doug. "We're celebrating. Stephanie has just agreed to make me the happiest man in the world. We just got engaged."

"Congratulations," Doug said and his sentiments were echoed by the others in the bar. Several of the women came and checked out Stephanie's ring, oohing and aahing over how beautiful it was.

"So does this mean you're retiring from the rodeo?" Doug asked.

"No. Not right now. I'll still be traveling for a while. But at some point, we will be buying a ranch in the valley. But you know what they say. Home is where the heart is and Stephanie is my home."

She smiled and waved a hand in front of her face. "Stop. You're going to make me cry."

"Never. I never want that. Not even happy tears."

Doug said, "Speaking of finding a home, thanks to you, Stephanie, Daphne Taylor was able to reunite with Maggie the dog. I wouldn't be surprised if they give that dog a key to the city at the Christmas tree lighting next month."

"Will you be in town for that?" Stephanie asked Geoff.

"Absolutely. It's our first Christmas together. I want to spend every moment of it with you."

"We're going to have the best holiday."

Geoff smiled. That was right. But this was only the beginning. They were going to have the best life.

* * * * *

WE HOPE YOU ENJOYED
THIS BOOK FROM

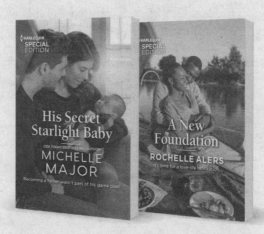

HARLEQUIN
SPECIAL
EDITION

Believe in love. Overcome obstacles. Find happiness.

Relate to finding comfort and strength in the
support of loved ones and enjoy the journey
no matter what life throws your way.

6 NEW BOOKS AVAILABLE EVERY MONTH!

#2875 DREAMING OF A CHRISTMAS COWBOY
Montana Mavericks: The Real Cowboys of Bronco Heights
by Brenda Harlen

In the Christmas play she wrote and will soon star in, Susanna Henry gets the guy. In real life, however, all-grown-up Susanna is no closer to hooking up with rancher Dean Abernathy than she was at seventeen. Until a sudden snowstorm strands them together overnight in a deserted theater...

#2876 SLEIGH RIDE WITH THE RANCHER
Men of the West • by Stella Bagwell

Sophia Vandale can't deny her attraction to rancher Colt Crawford, but when it comes to men, trusting her own judgment has only led to heartbreak. Maybe with a little Christmas magic she'll learn to trust her heart instead?

#2877 MERRY CHRISTMAS, BABY
Lovestruck, Vermont • by Teri Wilson

Every day is Christmas for holiday movie producer Candy Cane. But when she becomes guardian of her infant cousin, she's determined to rediscover the real thing. When she ends up snowed in with the local grinch, however, it might take a Christmas miracle to make the season merry...

#2878 THEIR TEXAS CHRISTMAS GIFT
Lockharts Lost & Found • by Cathy Gillen Thacker

Widow Faith Lockhart Hewitt is getting the ultimate Christmas gift in adopting an infant boy. But when the baby's father, navy SEAL lieutenant Zach Callahan, shows up, a marriage of convenience gives Faith a son and a husband! But she's already lost one husband and her second is about to be deployed. Can raising their son show them love is the only thing that matters?

#2879 CHRISTMAS AT THE CHÂTEAU
Bainbridge House • by Rochelle Alers

Viola Williamson's lifelong dream to run her own kitchen becomes a reality when she accepts the responsibility of executive chef at her family's hotel and wedding venue. What she doesn't anticipate is her attraction to the reclusive caretaker whose lineage is inexorably linked with the property known as Bainbridge House.

#2880 MOONLIGHT, MENORAHS AND MISTLETOE
Holliday, Oregon • by Wendy Warren

As a new landlord, Dr. Gideon Bowen is more irritating than ingratiating. Eden Berman should probably consider moving. But in the spirit of the holidays, Eden offers her friendship instead. As their relationship ignites, it's clear that Gideon is more mensch than menace. With each night of Hanukkah burning brighter, can Eden light his way to love?

*In the Christmas play she wrote and will soon star
in, Susanna Henry gets the guy. In real life, however,
all-grown-up Susanna is no closer to hooking up with
hardworking rancher Dean Abernathy than she was
at seventeen. Until a sudden snowstorm strands them
together overnight in a deserted theater…*

Read on for a sneak peek at
the final book in the Montana Mavericks:
The Real Cowboys of Bronco Heights continuity,
Dreaming of a Christmas Cowboy,
by Brenda Harlen!

"You're cold," Dean realized, when Susanna drew her
knees up to her chest and wrapped her arms around her
legs, no doubt trying to conserve her own body heat as
she huddled under the blanket draped over her shoulders
like a cape.

"A little," she admitted.

"Come here," he said, patting the space on the floor
beside him.

She hesitated for about half a second before scooting
over, obviously accepting that sharing body heat was the
logical thing to do.

But as she snuggled against him, her head against
his shoulder, her curvy body aligned with his, there was
suddenly more heat coursing through his veins than Dean

had anticipated. And maybe it was the normal reaction for a man in close proximity to an attractive woman, but this was *Susanna*.

He wasn't supposed to be thinking of Susanna as an attractive woman—or a woman at all.

She was a friend.

Almost like a sister.

But she's not your sister, a voice in the back of his head reminded him. *So there's absolutely no reason you can't kiss her.*

Don't do it, the rational side of his brain pleaded. *Kissing Susanna will change everything.*

Change is good. Necessary, even.

When Susanna tipped her head back to look at him, obviously waiting for a response to something she'd said, all he could think about was the fact that her lips were *right there*. That barely a few scant inches separated his mouth from hers.

He only needed to dip his head and he could taste those sweetly curved lips that had tempted him for so long, despite all of his best efforts to pretend it wasn't true.

Not that he had any intention of breaching that distance.

Of course not.

Because this was *Susanna*.

No way would he ever—

Apparently the signals from his brain didn't make it to his mouth, because it was already brushing over hers.

Don't miss
Dreaming of a Christmas Cowboy *by Brenda Harlen,
available December 2021 wherever
Harlequin Special Edition books and ebooks are sold.*

Harlequin.com

Get 4 FREE REWARDS!

We'll send you 2 FREE Books plus 2 FREE Mystery Gifts.

Harlequin Special Edition books relate to finding comfort and strength in the support of loved ones and enjoying the journey no matter what life throws your way.

FREE
Value Over
$20

YES! Please send me 2 FREE Harlequin Special Edition novels and my 2 FREE gifts (gifts are worth about $10 retail). After receiving them, if I don't wish to receive any more books, I can return the shipping statement marked "cancel." If I don't cancel, I will receive 6 brand-new novels every month and be billed just $4.99 per book in the U.S. or $5.74 per book in Canada. That's a savings of at least 12% off the cover price! It's quite a bargain! Shipping and handling is just 50¢ per book in the U.S. and $1.25 per book in Canada.* I understand that accepting the 2 free books and gifts places me under no obligation to buy anything. I can always return a shipment and cancel at any time. The free books and gifts are mine to keep no matter what I decide.

235/335 HDN GNMP

Name (please print)

Address   Apt. #

City   State/Province   Zip/Postal Code

Email: Please check this box ☐ if you would like to receive newsletters and promotional emails from Harlequin Enterprises ULC and its affiliates. You can unsubscribe anytime.

Mail to the **Harlequin Reader Service:**
IN U.S.A.: P.O. Box 1341, Buffalo, NY 14240-8531
IN CANADA: P.O. Box 603, Fort Erie, Ontario L2A 5X3

Want to try 2 free books from another series! Call 1-800-873-8635 or visit www.ReaderService.com.

SPECIAL EXCERPT FROM

HQN

*Angi Guilardi needs a man for Christmas—at least,
according to her mother. Balancing work and her
eight-year-old son, she has no time for romance...until
Angi runs into Gabriel Carlyle. Temporarily helping at
his grandmother's flower shop, Gabriel doesn't plan
to stick around, especially after he bumps into Angi,
one of his childhood bullies. But with their undeniable
chemistry, they're both finding it hard to stay away from
each other...*

Read on for a sneak preview of
Mistletoe Season,
the next book in USA TODAY *bestselling author
Michelle Major's Carolina Girls series,
available October 2021!*

"Who's dating?" Josie, who sat in the front row, leaned forward in her chair.

"No one," Gabe said through clenched teeth.

"Not even a little." Angi offered a patently fake smile. "I'd be thrilled to work with Gabe. I'm sure he'll have lots to offer as far as making this Christmas season in Magnolia the most festive ever."

The words seemed benign enough on the surface, but Gabe knew a challenge when he heard one.

"I have loads of time to devote to this town," he said solemnly, placing a hand over his chest. He glanced down at Josie and her cronies and gave his most winsome smile. "I know it will make my grandma happy."

As expected, the women clucked and cooed over his devotion. Angi looked like she wanted to reach around Malcolm and scratch out Gabe's eyes, and it was strangely satisfying to get under her skin.

"Well, then." Mal grabbed each of their hands and held them above his head like some kind of referee calling a heavyweight boxing match. "We have our new Christmas on the Coast power couple."

Don't miss
Mistletoe Season by Michelle Major,
available October 2021 wherever HQN books
and ebooks are sold.

HQNBooks.com